Begin Again

Available in print and digital formats online at amazon.com

Copyright © 2013 – C Clef Publishing

All rights reserved. No part of this publication may be reproduced, stored in a retrieval system, or transmitted, in any form or by any means, electronic, mechanical, photocopying, recording, or otherwise, without prior written permission from the author.

This is fictional work, and all names, characters, and incidents depicted herein, are real only in the author's imagination. Any similarities to persons living or dead, or events past or present, are pure coincidence.

Book Design: Mike Fontenot

Cover Design: Mike Fontenot

Front Cover Image: Alexander Karnes
(http://steamby51.deviantart.com)

Printing History:

Original – December 2013

First Revision – August 2016

Hard Cover – October 2015

PRINTED IN THE UNITED STATES OF AMERICA

ISBN-13: 9781491067574

ISBN-10: 1491067578

10 9 8 7 6 5 4 3 2 1

"We are, and always will be — no matter what paths we travel, or what complications life throws at us — **Audio Distortion...**"

~Catrin Meredith

prologue

10:30 AM – Tuesday – Torino, Italy

Emma Greene

"Buongiorno, Emma!" the girl behind the counter calls out.

"E a voi, Bianca," I reply.

After a brief silence, I turn to look at her, and find a face covered in confusion.

"What's with the face?"

"It is Tuesday…"

I laugh.

"I was passing by, and my heart pulled me in. You know me and music…"

I hear her laugh, as I start to wander down my favorite aisle, but a second prolonged silence, and Bianca's unusual seriousness, makes me pull up short. I turn and walk back to the front counter, where I find her intently staring at me.

"What's going on? You're never this serious…"

"A very odd thing has happened this morning… and now, your random appearance…"

"Stranger than me just turning up in your shop one day, and you recognizing me immediately?" I ask with a smile.

"Perhaps it is. I will leave it to you to decide…" she replies, reaching under her counter and getting something. "A courier left this an hour ago…"

She hands me a square cardboard envelope that I recognize as a CD mailer. The moment I see that it's *addressed to me*, I understand her confusion.

"How is this possible?" I ask.

"As you told me when we first met, because no one knows you are here, I too, was quite confused. My concern that it may be important, forced me to sign for it, rather than send it back."

I glance at the address of origin, and see that it was sent from Ibiza, Spain.

"Well… I assure you I don't know anyone in Ibiza, *and* not even my closest friends know I am here."

"Well then," Bianca says, walking over, locking the door, and turning off the small neon OPEN sign, "I would suggest you open it and we investigate…"

forty-six hours later
8:30 AM – Thursday – Torino, Italy

I'm standing outside the door when Marco and Bianca arrive to open their store.

"Emma, it is quite early. Is there some problem?" Bianca asks.

"No… no problem. But… I do need a favor guys – a big favor."

"But of course, Emma, anything!"

"Remember the CD you gave me Tuesday?"

"Of course," Bianca replies, unlocking the door. "Do you wish to know who recorded the song?"

"Not yet. I did discover a hidden mp3 file on the disk – it's a recorded message – and now I know *why* I got it," I reply, following them into the store.

"Really? May I ask what it says?" Bianca asks, as she locks the door behind us. Marco goes about turning things on, and getting the store ready for business.

I pull the CD out of my notebook, and stare at it for a moment... thinking.

"I'll let you hear the message, in return for the favor... well two actually..."

"It sounds very... very..." Marco says from across the room, looking at his sister, "what is the word in English?"

"Di malaugurio?" Bianca asks, a bit spooked.

"Si...si..."

I raise my eyebrows, and Bianca understands my visual request for a translation.

"Ominous..."

"What do you need?" Marco asks, stopping next to us.

"I need to make four copies of the song on the CD, and I need a contact – *in Spain* – who can ship them overnight for me..."

Finally Bianca relaxes, and laughs. Marco is quick to follow.

"Come," Marco says, turning toward his office. "Rico has a small store in Santa Pola – a town near Alicante. We trade with him regularly, and he thinks Bianca is 'cute', and will do anything for her..."

He makes Bianca blush, and me laugh.

"I will send him the file, have him make copies, and send them where ever you wish them to go."

Still laughing, I follow them into their office...

four days later
9:00 AM – Monday – Southport, England

Catrin Meredith

"Miss Meredith," my new assistant says, sticking her head in my door, "A courier just dropped this off for you. I told him you were here, but he insisted I could sign for it."

"Shannon... I thought we talked about the whole 'Miss' thing..." I say, frowning and waving her into the office. "We're within five months of each other age wise – you really should be calling me Cadi, like everyone else does. We're in a concert hall... not a court room."

When she makes it to my desk, she's as red as a fire engine, and quickly hands me what appears to be a CD mailer. As I am reading the addresses on the front, Martha appears at the door.

"Good morning MISS MEREDITH!"

Again, poor Shannon blushes.

"Now... see what you've started?"

"What's that?" Martha asks, "I saw the truck driving off."

"No idea," I reply, "but it came from Santa Pola, Spain – where I know no one."

"I'll be at the front desk," Shannon says, and quickly disappears out the door.

"Don't worry, Cadi... she'll loosen up. Just give her some time. After all, it isn't everyday someone gets hired by the bass player for one of music's biggest pop bands..."

I laugh, pull the tab to open the envelope, and find only an unlabeled CD inside...

five hours later
9:00 AM – Monday – Lake Tahoe, California

Emily Táo

Because I'm not expecting anyone, when I hear the chime on the lobby door, I get up from my desk and head out front. I arrive in our small lobby at the same time my husband does, to find an overnight courier standing there with a clipboard.

"Ms Emily Táo?"

"Not any more... but I was once," I reply, making Leonard laugh.

When the guy looks confused, I explain.

"I got married, that's all. Whacha got anyhow?"

He holds up a white cardboard CD mailer.

"Just this... but I need a signature."

"No problem. You want it as addressed?

"Well..."

I laugh, take his electronic signature pad, and scribble Emily Táo, for the first time in years. He smiles, hands me the cardboard mailer, and disappears out the door.

"Santa Pola, Spain?" I mumble, pulling the tab, and tearing it open.

"You know someone in Spain?" Leonard asks, watching intently.

"Nope... not that I know of..." I reply, as I pull a single, unlabeled CD, out of the mailer.

"Well... fortunately for you, I just happen to have a CD player handy," he says, laughing and holding open the door to the studio...

thirty minutes later
10:30 AM – Monday – Fort Collins, Colorado

Stanley Campbell

When we hear "Mr. Campbell," over the classroom intercom, all my students go quiet.

"Yes, Theresa?" I reply.

"I just signed for an overnight package from a courier service, address to you here at the school. I'm sending it down with a student."

"Thanks, Theresa!"

I turn back to face my class.

"Okay… so… clefs… someone tell me which ones we commonly use."

"Bass clef!" one student calls out.

"Treble clef," comes from another.

"And time signatures?" I ask.

"4/4 is most common," a girl in the front row replies.

"Very good – you guys were paying attention."

A student appears at the door, knocks, and I tell her to come in. She crosses the room, hands me a white CD mailer, I thank her and she goes back to the office.

As I stand reading the return address, I realize everyone is sitting quietly, watching me.

"Do you guys know anyone in Santa Pola, Spain?"

Most of them laugh, and a few mumble, 'huh'?

"Yeah… me neither."

I pull the small tab to open the mailer and find a blank CD inside.

"So… what say we find out what's on it guys?" I say, walking over and popping it into a portable player I keep in the classroom.

With 16 pairs of eyes watching, I push play...

thirty minutes later
10:00 AM – Monday – Los Angeles, California

Willie Morgan

I'm carefully mixing a track for a new artist, when the door to the booth opens, and one of the many secretaries in the building sticks her head in.

"Sorry to interrupt, Willie..." she whispers.

"No need to whisper, Carrie, the mics are off. What's up?"

"This just came for you. Richard said I should bring it down."

She holds out a cardboard CD mailer, which I take from her.

"I didn't know you had friends in Spain," she says, smiling.

"I don't... that I know of," I reply, spinning it around so I can read the origin address.

"Well... see ya later. Gotta get back to work."

She lets the door go, crosses the studio and disappears out the door. Now curious, I pull the tab on the mailer, tear it open, and find a blank CD with no explanation inside.

With a shrug, I slip it into the nearest CD drive, and click 'play'...

one

Stanley

I'm lost in the lyrics, handwritten on the page in my hands, when my dad walks up.

"Hey guy – why so serious?"

"Lyrics..." I reply, holding up the page.

"Oh..." He pauses for a moment, and then sits down next to me, on the steps. "You okay?"

"I guess..."

When I sit silently staring at the page in my hand, my dad continues.

"I stopped by to tell you that I have a crew that can handle the modifications to your house, in four days. You interested?"

"Well..."

"Still not sure you want to do it?"

I frown, confirming what he's suspected for months – my mind is still stuck on Emma... and the possibility she'll come back.

"Four years, Stanley – it's been just more than four years since the two of you 'broke up'. I know what I said the day I 'lectured' the four of you, right after she left, but this has gone past all that. When are you going to quit screwing around, and do what needs to be done?"

"We've been over this, Dad... repeatedly. I can't *make* her do anything. No one except Emma, can make Emma do anything."

"Good point, son. But you can damn sure make *Stanley* do something..."

"I don't even know where she is..." I start to say, and then jump when my dad snatches the envelope I'm holding, out of my hand.

"You could start here," he replies, pointing at the postmark on the envelope...

I-10123
Torino Italy

I take the envelope back, and sit staring at it.

"How long are you going to continue to torture yourself, Stan?"

"We decided, Dad... we decided that what we had wasn't meant to be permanent."

"Yeah... right. Two twenty-one year olds, trying to find their way, in a high-pressure world, of bright lights and fame," he says, looking at me, and shaking his head.

"May I?" he asks, reaching for the single sheet of paper I'm holding, which I let go of.

I watch quietly, as he reads the five stanzas of lyrics she's written, and as he hands it back to me, he says, "If you don't go find her, you can bet I'm going to. 'Daughter-in-law or *daughter*' as I recall, which means..."

He's interrupted by my current 'girlfriend' as she comes out the door behind us.

"Hey, Stan – I'm off to work."

"Okay," I reply, standing up and kissing her. "Do you want to meet us for dinner, or should I come and get you?"

"I can get there."

The moment she glances at what's in my hand, a brief look of depression sweeps over her face, telling me she knows what it is. After a second, she smiles, and looks at my dad.

"It's really nice of you to do the 'birthday dinner' thing for me, Mr. Campbell."

"It's my pleasure, Courtney. Logan also has a gift for you – which she and Georgie came up with. Hopefully, whatever it is, it doesn't embarrass you."

"I'm sure it will be perfect."

She gives me another quick kiss, and disappears down the driveway, to her car, which is parked on the street.

"She knows," I mumble, sitting back down next to my dad.

"Of course she does. She's just waiting for you to admit it. You know she doesn't deserve this…"

Sure, he's right, but it isn't something I want to talk about.

"I have to get to school, Dad. Let's hold off on the project for now, okay?"

"Sure kid. I'll see you at dinner tonight."

"Okay… see you then," I reply, as I head for my truck.

Just as I have for the last few months, all the way to the high school, I think about just one thing…

More accurately, *about just one person…*

two
Emma

A SUNNY MORNING
ON A QUAINT AND QUIET SIDE STREET
TORINO, ITALY

It's Thursday – *Music Day*.

This is my fourth trip to *'Musica Riciclata'* – or *Recycled Music* – a small place less than a mile from where I now live. They sell new and used CDs, and while browsing, I've even stumbled across some very old vinyl, and, believe it or not, some 8-track tapes!

Although I haven't been a musician or performer for quite some time, I still have this weird need to keep up with it. So, every Thursday for the last two years, no matter where I've been, I find a music store – and I browse.

Destiny seems, for whatever reasons, unwilling to allow me to let go of my past.

INSIDE 'MUSICA RICICLATA'

"Buongiorno, Emma!" Bianca calls out.

"E a voi, Bianca," I reply.

Bianca and her brother Marco own 'Musica Riciclata'. She's the only person in town who knows who I actually am. I was kind of shocked when, within thirty seconds of my arrival the first time I was here, she recognized me. Her brother thought she was nuts – until I showed him my passport...

Over time, I've actually gotten comfortable being 'anonymous'...

You see, *Audio Distortion*, like every other 'pop-music phenomenon', eventually faded. For about a year, *Journeys End* was heard *everywhere*. During the second year, all our songs slipped in play rotations around the world, mostly because we had pretty much disappeared off the face of the earth. After two full years, while we do still pop up on digital stations online, and satellite radio, it's not very often. I've even overheard conversations where someone has said, *'...I don't know what happened to Audio Distortion...'*

We were quickly replaced by a German pop band – appropriately name *Nächste Seite* – or in English, *Next Page*. They were a bunch of bored college kids who got together and recorded a single song in a dorm room – and ended up at the top of the European singles charts four weeks later. Once they recorded the song in English, they stormed the rest of the world's singles charts as well.

Staying true to their roots, they always record their songs in both German and English. Their first CD titled *Turning*, made it to number one – on almost every chart – in four weeks. And everyone said *our* rise was meteoric?

And, as is the way of the music world, it took less than six months for *Next Page*'s nemesis to appear – yet another group of American high school kids...

TWO YEARS AGO
SOMEWHERE IN KANSAS

They call themselves *Ransom* – which is actually the name of the town in Kansas where they were discovered. I always found it interesting that, no matter how much pressure was put on them by the record company they eventually signed with, they staunchly refused to change their name to 'something a bit more catchy'.

I'm pretty sure that was Emily's doing...

Yep, that's right. Emily and Willie found them, on one of their many jaunts around the country, visiting high schools. An old college friend of Ms. Dreesen called and told her about them, and she in turn told Emily and Willie. Two weeks later Discovery Studios gave a presentation for the music students at Western Plains High School. After school the same day, Willie and Emily wandered into the small music room while the kids were playing – and the chemistry was amazing. It was so reminiscent of five kids in a pizzeria, that it gave them goose bumps.

Over the next few days, Emily and Willie spoke one-on-one to each of the kids, then with them as a group one afternoon. Finally, after their own intense discussion, they sat the five kids down together, and told them that if they were interested, Discovery Studios wanted the chance to work with them. The kids, of course, pretty much freaked.

Although the kids were very good musicians, none of them was really a vocalist – something Emily and Willie discussed at length. Fact was, they needed a singer...

Then, the magic happened.

As fate would have it, Emily found one, on the way to her rental car, as she and Willie were headed for the airport. The moment she heard the voice, she stopped dead in her tracks, causing the music teacher to almost knock her down, when she ran into her. Emily turned toward the sound, and her eyes came to rest on a petite young girl, sitting under a big tree, books open in front of her, *singing.*

Needless to say, she and Willie postponed their departure, and over the next week, *Ransom* became a band.

With the help of the music teacher, they got the six of them together, and the results were amazing. Emily and Willie were more than a bit stunned.

Once school was out for the summer, Discovery Studios flew the kids – and a couple of parents – out to Tahoe. Emily took charge, and put the kids to work the moment they walked into the studio. Willie even mentioned how amusing it was, watching Emily deal with... well... *herself!* Apparently, the band's bass player was the new Emily Táo – a hardheaded, consummate, pain in the...

It took them – with Stanley's on-and-off help, and six separate trips to the studio – about six months to turn six kids, first into a band, and then into the next musical 'phenomenon'.

They came to me, a few weeks before I embarked on what is now a life adventure, with a request...

TWENTY-TWO MONTHS AGO
INSIDE DISCOVERY STUDIOS

"We need you talk to each of them Emma, and then write their title song," Emily said.

"Catch is," came from Stan – who was grinning like a Cheshire cat – "it has to be a ballad."

"You want to launch a pop band, with a *ballad*?" I asked, more than a bit mystified.

"Insane, right?" Emily replied, laughing. "Trust me, the moment you meet them, you'll get it..."

It may have been a totally crazy idea, but the results would turn out to be far more amazing than any of us could have imagined.

Emily was right – within seconds of meeting the kids, I understood what she and Stan were trying to do. When I asked the kids how they felt about their first song being a ballad, the drummer laughed, pointed at the lead singer, and said, "You should hear her sing *Destined to Be*..." When the singer blushed, and the bass player giggled, I knew it would work.

After multiple conversations with the kids, I discovered there was a stressed 'relationship' going on between one of them, and someone back home.

How lucky could I get? One of the things I've become intimately familiar with, and am *very good* at writing about is emotional confusion.

Although the kid in question wasn't willing to discuss things openly, a compromise was reached – I could write about it, if I didn't use names.

It took me three days of quiet contemplation, solitude, and a number of erasers, to write the lyrics. The song's theme is the inability we sometimes experience, when trying to break someone's hold on our heart... even though we know it needs to be done.

Once I was satisfied with what I had, I immediately went and let the band member in question read it. Although there were a few tears, I was eventually given permission to use it, *and* a very passionate hug. I asked about a title, and was told 'I need to think about it...'

One at a time, I let the other kids read it, and the thing I found totally intriguing, was that every single one of them knew exactly what – *and who* – it was about...

Seems 'friendship' hadn't changed much since I was in high school.

When Emily finally read it, the tears came when she got to the chorus. I gave her and Willie a few ideas for tempo, and they went to work with the band, while I spent the next two days with their lead singer – a fifteen year old named Misty.

Although she had no formal training, it was blatantly apparent she had a voice easily as good as mine. She captured the essence of the lyrics the first time she sang them, and at one point, even got teary-eyed. Truth is, she surprised even me.

On the second day, Misty and I were sitting at the water's edge, discussing the difference in the volume and tone of the 'chest' and 'head' voices, when the lead guitarist walked up, handed me a folded piece of paper, then turned and went back into the studio. I opened it and found a single handwritten word in the center...

hostage

I smiled, mumbled "perfect", and handed it to Misty. She too smiled, and said, "It is..."

After two more months of intense practice and rehearsal, Willie and Emily decided it was time for the kids to record. I'm not sure who was more amped – the kids, or their parents.

The day they made their first attempt, it took them multiple tries – which caused the drummer and lead guitarist some undue stress, but Willie and Emily talked them through it. It took them a week, but they eventually pulled it off – and the results were nothing short of amazing.

Once they had a clean digital master of the song, Emily tried to convince them to put it up for free, online. When they were hesitant, Stan spoke up...

"You guys do remember *Audio Distortion*, right?"

"Well... of course," Misty replied.

"Well guys, she..." Stan added, pointing directly at Emily, who was sitting on the front edge of her desk, "...is the one who single-handedly started, and launched our band."

"Without Emily, and her insane ideas," Willie volunteered, "you wouldn't be here now... doing what you are doing. None of this..." he waved his arms to indicate the studio, "...would exist."

"Guys..." Emily said, sliding off her desk, crossing the room to the kids and squatting down in front of them, using Misty's knee to balance herself, "If you will trust me on this, you will end up right where I think you want to. We..." she smiled, and pointed at Stan and Willie with her free hand, "...had our turn. We've put all this effort into you guys, because we believe it's now *your* turn."

The kids turned to look at one another, and after a few moments of contemplation, each nodded their understanding.

And of course, in the end, the kids *and* their parents agreed to do it Emily's way. The totally amusing part came when, less than seventy-two hours after they put it up, the silly thing went viral.

Between the kid's small website, and the Discovery Studios website (both of which crashed from the insane traffic levels), the song was downloaded over 15,000 times the first week it was posted. By the end of the second week, it broke the 50,000 mark. I'm pretty sure every teenager on the planet, that had suffered a broken heart, had it on their mp3 player...

Richard called Emily the moment he heard about it, and proceeded to give her a huge butt-chewing, asking why she hadn't brought them directly to him.

Emily laughed and told him they were on their way, with a rough demo of the first CD, and a bunch of parents in tow.

Six months later, their first CD hit the charts, and within days, ended up directly below *Turning,* which at the time, was number one. The kids decided to use the ballad's title for the CD's title – with a twist.

Over their name, they put **PAID** and it looked like someone had stamped it! Across the bottom of the image was the word *hostage,* in lower case, and in handwriting that matched the note I was given.

Emily and Willie thought it was ingenious.

Ransom and *Next Page* spent the following year, taking turns at the top.

While *Audio Distortion* may have disbanded, the members were still very much, a continuous presence in the world of music.

Well... most of them were...

BACK INSIDE 'MUSICA RICICLATA'

"I'll take these three."

I put a new copy, of the English version, of *Next Page*'s most recent CD on the counter, along with a used copy of 'Buoni o Cattivi' by Vasco – an Italian rock singer – and an old Xavier Nadoo CD from the 80s. Some might find it odd, since I don't speak Italian, but for me, it's been more about *the music*... than the lyrics.

Once a week, a past I can't seem to escape, shows itself...

"You know, if you will bring back the ones you purchased last time, I will give you a credit," Bianca offers, as she goes about ringing up the purchase.

"I know... and I might do that eventually. You *will* let me know when *Ransom*'s new CD gets here, right?"

"Of course," she replies with a laugh, "I have ordered three copies, and one is reserved for you."

She puts the CDs into a small bag, then hesitates a moment and again makes eye contact with me.

"And what of your phantom CD? Did the copies arrive as planned?"

I laugh.

"Only time will tell, Bianca. If I know them as well as I think I do, they have probably already rearranged it. I've been diligently working on some lyrics... as the 'voice' suggested."

"Well, I will be excited to hear them, if you feel the need to share. Will I see you next Thursday?"

"Probably," I reply, following it with a laugh. "Might be sooner if that CD comes in. And... you will be the only one who gets to read them – when the time comes."

She actually blushes.

"Well, I suggest you come at noon next week, and have lunch with Marco and me. We will waste the afternoon discussing music!"

"See ya!"

Twenty minutes later, I'm once again, under my favorite tree in the park, using my laptop to load the CDs into my iPod. Once I'm done, instead playing one of them, I search until I find the hidden file I copied from the 'phantom CD'. I stare at the iPod for a few seconds, then push play, and immediately the intriguing, deep male voice begins ...

Miss Greene... I have sent you the enclosed CD with a purpose.

The song was written many years ago... by myself, and a very close friend, for a record we produced together. It was a time in our lives when we were experimenting... and searching... just as you are now.

While I am certain you could search and determine who I am, I am in hopes you will not feel the need to do so. Who I am is not important. What is important is the favor I would ask of you.

Add lyrics to the melody. The subject I will leave entirely to you, for having heard many of your songs, I am certain you will come up with something spectacular. Although I know there is great difference between your music and mine, I believe all music is universal, and I am certain you can do this with minimal changes to the song.

I will contact you again soon, with a full explanation.

three

Catrin

My journey in search of myself has produced some interesting results. I've decided I am in fact, a bit of a conglomeration. Yes, my roots and heritage are unquestionably Welsh, but I have discovered I am very much British as well. And of course, four years of constant exposure have served to make me a good bit American too. Because I hold tightly to my heritage, my parents have fully accepted the path I've chosen to travel – one that includes all of my acculturations.

Because I'm bigger on comfortable, than I am on style, with the exception of performances with the orchestra, and family gatherings, Cadi Meredith can be found in jeans, sneakers, and a ponytail. Should I ever decide to go back to my pigtails, a haircut will be mandatory, as it has grown out considerably in the last couple of years.

While I do still play violin regularly, I've also moved on to managing the orchestra's operation. When Leonard and Emily got married, he moved on – to Lake Tahoe. So, in order to support myself (yeah, the band made some money, and no, I haven't squandered all of mine), I went back to school and got a minor degree in business administration – so my resume will at least appear legitimate. For me, working is more about being useful, than about getting rich.

While I have dated, I'm still single. I'm okay with that. I think that maybe I'm waiting for the same magic that occurred the day Emily and Lenny met...

I'm only twenty-five... I have time.

This morning, a group of orchestra members are discussing our next performance – a fundraiser to help a local private school. As I listen, I'm scanning the suggested playlist, when something catches my eye.

"Say... isn't this," I ask, tapping on the page in my hand, "a song from the Batman movie?"

Martha laughs, and says, "It was part of the soundtrack, yes, but it wasn't written for the movie."

As I stand, reading the music, out of nowhere, a thought pops into my head. I turn to the nearest computer, do a quick search, and once I find what I'm after, smile, and turn to the others.

"What are we doing about the lyrics?"

"We intend to perform it instrumentally. Why?"

"Guys, I have the most amazingly crazy idea..."

Fate and destiny, once again...

four

Catrin

"Stanley, it's me…"

"Hey, Cadi! Been a while. What's up in England?"

"I need to ask you something…"

"Shoot."

"Where's Emma?"

"Not sure. I received some new lyrics from her a few days ago, and the envelope was post marked Torino, Italy. And, as usual, it has no return address."

"I want to get a hold of her – how can I do it?"

"Short of going and searching the entire city of Torino, I have no idea. Except for sending me lyrics, she hasn't felt the need to communicate with any of us yet. Logan and I are still checking on her house, paying the power bill, and having the yard maintained. I've even gone as far as letting Georgia drive her Jeep – so I don't have to keep going over and starting it once a week. And, each time I get mail, it's either just before she leaves a place or right after she arrives. I've never gotten two from the same place."

"Damn…"

"What's going on, Cadi?"

"I needed her for… something. Maybe, I was just hoping…"

"Being kinda cryptic, aren't ya?"

"I was going to ask her to sing with the orchestra… that's all. I came across something in one of our recital playlists, and it struck me that her voice would be perfect…"

"Well, my dad has decided it may be time to find her, but I'm not sure what his plan is. I keep thinking about what he said to us, right after she left…"

"Yeah, me too. But damn it, Stanley, she's had enough time. I want my friend back."

"You and me both, Cadi… honest to God…"

"So… that issue aside, how's life in Fort Collins?"

"Hot, actually. They've talked me into Summer School for the first time, so I'm working here and not getting much done on the house. I've been writing – Richard called about some stuff for a new artist they are picking up. And believe it or not, Nickelodeon wants me to write a song for one of their shows."

"Oh how cool!"

"What about you then?"

"Same old stuff. Life in the slow lane – which I am completely fine with."

"Have you fallen in love yet?"

"Yeah, right. I'm holding out for my Emily-Lenny moment."

"Yeah, I know that feeling girl…"

"Huh? I thought you and…"

"Long story."

"Oh…"

There is a strained silence for a few seconds, and then I try to recover the moment.

"I sent her a birthday card."

"She got it – and laughed. Dad is doing the dinner thing for her tonight."

"And?"

"And, she asked if I would mind if she went home to Boston for her actual birthday – so I bought her a ticket."

"I feel like I should say something... but I can only come up with one thing, Stan – and I'm thinking it's not something you want to hear..."

"Oh, relax, Cadi... I've been saying it myself – repeatedly – for the last couple of weeks."

Again, there is a weird, pressured silence. Then, in a bizarrely intriguing twist, we say the same thing, *at the exact same time...*

"Fate and destiny..."

five
Stanley

Having finished my call with Cadi, I take a seat on a small retaining wall, outside the rehearsal room. Although I was hesitant, I'm finding that teaching a summer class has its benefits. The kids are here because they want to be – not because they have to be. I find it amusing that although summer days are only four hours, I inevitably end up staying all day.

Although totally lost in thought, after a few moments, the musician in me wins out, and I turn my attention to the music inside the room. I immediately know my sophomores are trying to 'copy' something. What catches my attention is the tempo – although I'm fairly certain, it's just a standard 4/4 beat, something about it makes it sound a lot faster.

Now concentrating on the music, I stand up and go inside. Halfway across the room, Pete and Patty see me coming, and quickly stop what they're doing.

"Guys... what's up with that?"

"We know how you feel about audibly copying..." Patty replies, looking a bit guilty.

"Why not get the sheet music?"

"We have it," Pete says, holding up some pages, "but it's kind of confusing."

I take the pages when he holds them out to me, and start reading.

"Prozzäk?" I mumble.

"Yeah – it's some band my dad really likes."

"Gonna play it for him?"

"That's what we're thinking," Patty replies, "when we play the Summer Celebration, at the end of the month."

When I look at her, I see the frown on her face.

"What?"

"I told Pete, I think that... well... it's beyond us."

"Nothing is beyond you, Patty – it just requires a little extra effort. From what I just heard, it sounds fast guys, but I'm pretty sure it's just a 4/4 tempo. You have the whole song?"

"Yes, sir."

"Hit play, let's listen..."

I take a seat, and start reading the music, not really paying any attention to the lyrics. A couple of the shifts I find in the middle of the song make me immediately understand what their problem is, and give me what could be an entertaining solution as well.

Emily and Willie.

Deep down, they've always been 'speed demons' where music is concerned. However, they always seemed to control themselves, whenever we were playing, or creating, *Audio Distortion* music. More than once over the years, I walked in and found them shredding some speed metal of some kind – because they could. Either one of them could help the kids, with the concept of tempo shifts.

I spin around, and as the music starts, I do a quick search to find out who the musicians are. It turns out to be a sort of alternative pop group from Canada – which I've actually never heard of. After some reading, I discover the *musicians* are *animated* – which makes me laugh.

By the second stanza, about fifteen kids who filtered in from the halls, are dancing around the room, laughing. The fact the song was recorded before most of them had even started school, lends credence to my belief that music is indeed, universal.

Then, I hear the hook… and am instantly awash with goose bumps.

I'm about to close the website, when, for reasons unknown, I click on one more link… and up pops a single image, of the two cartoon characters designed to depict the musicians. Below the picture is a caption…

> '…*images of Prozzäk's heroes, Simon and Milo – one love sick and the other oblivious to anything but the music*'.

Yeah… the fact that, at one point in our lives, it would have described me and Emma perfectly, pretty much weirds me out.

Damn you, Emma Greene… I think to myself, and laugh.

six

Stanley

"Morgan."

"Do you always answer your phone like that?"

"Of course I do. I'm an engineer, not a 'suit'."

"Been banging on those drums lately?"

"Well... yeah. But Bailey spends more time on them than I do anymore. If she keeps it up, she'll probably turn into an awesome drummer."

"Like father, like daughter, dude."

"So... what's up?"

"I need your expertise. I have a couple of kids who are trying to cover a song, and it has some fairly complex tempo shifts, that are kicking their butts. I figured the world's best drummer could help them pull it off."

"Who are they trying to cover?"

"Group from about fifteen years ago, called Prozzäk. I'd never heard of them..."

"I have – alternative dance club stuff. Was pretty catchy as I recall."

"So, think you can get away for a couple days? I know Vicki is getting close again..."

"I'll have to ask her. Good thing is, her mom is right there in town, and she loves spending time with Bailey."

"Well, get back to me after you talk to your wife."

"I'll see what I can do. Would be nice to 'help' again. Haven't been in that environment since... well..."

"Yeah, I know Willie. I'm beginning to miss it all too. Call me later – I gotta get back to class."

"Later dude."

I close the phone, open the door to the rehearsal room, and as fate would have it, hear the hook that moments earlier, reached out and, for some unknown reason, grabbed my heart…

w w w dot
I won't believe it
w w w dot
Until I read it
My heart is tied up in a knot
You know it's true
w w w dot **nevergetoveryou**

There… I admitted it, even if only to myself.

That woman and I are about to take this to its inevitable conclusion – after all, she's the one who's always stirring up the fate and destiny.

Then… in the middle of my 'moment', Courtney pops into my head, and although I expect pangs of guilt to begin jabbing me – they don't.

Thing is, I'm not in love with Courtney, and I know that. And, according to my dad, she knows it too.

I am… and have always been, very much in love, with Emma Greene – regardless of what we may have 'decided', years ago.

"Sometimes, Stanley Campbell," I mumble to myself, as I sit down at my desk, "you can be such a huge dweeb…"

seven

Willie

"How are the two most beautiful girls in the world today?"

"*Daddy!*" my daughter yells, as she races over, and jumps into my arms.

"Hey, husband. How are things in the world of music today?"

"An interesting question, actually. Stan called me this morning…"

I lean over, and kiss my very pregnant wife.

"How's he doing?"

"I dunno. Something's up – something other than what he called about. I could tell."

"What did he want?"

"Me to come over, and help a couple of his kids…"

"Wow! That's kinda cool. When are we going?"

"Victoria, you're eight months pregnant – I'm not going to drop everything, and rush to Fort Collins, just because Stanley asked me to."

"Why not? You always have before…" she replies, giving me a seriously devious smile.

When I do nothing more than stare at her, definitely shocked by her response, she continues.

"You do remember our vows, right? *'Our lives will merge…'* is what we said. I told you that I would never get between you and music – and I meant it. Why do you think I tolerate *that child,*" she pauses, and with a big smile, points at Bailey, who is still in my arms, "constantly beating on your drums? On a number of occasions, when an assignment was 'hot', and I had to fly at the drop of a hat, you stepped up, Willie. Without a word, you took responsibility for a baby, and our lives in general, and sent me on my way – because you know what writing means to me."

She pauses again, walks over, and puts a hand on my cheek.

"I know what music means to you. *It is you*... and it always will be. Stan needs you, it's about music... when do we leave, babe?"

Yes, I did in fact manage to marry the most perfect woman on the planet...

"You're sure?"

"Yes, I am. But we're driving. We'll have to stop a lot, but I'm not taking the chance this baby will enter the world at 35,000 feet, in an airplane."

"Do you want to go see Grandma and Grandpa, Bailey?"

I squat down, stand my daughter up in front of me, and then pull my cell out of my pocket.

"And... while we're there, Daddy is gonna make some music..."

The moment she hears 'make music', Bailey bolts for the drum set in the family room and even before I finish dialing, she is on the stool, pounding away.

Victoria rolls her eyes, and disappears back into the kitchen.

eight

Willie

"Emily – it's Willie. You got a sec?"

"Heck yeah! What's the world's best drummer up to?"

"Scheming – what else?"

"Bet you need my help…"

"Lucky guess," I reply, laughing. "What's your schedule look like?"

"Nothing too exciting. Richard has his latest discovery here…"

"So that's where he disappeared to…" I mumble.

"We're trying to turn them into a band – instead of five individuals…"

"And how's that working so far?"

"*Do not* irritate me, Morgan… You aren't *that* far away."

Over the years, Emily and I made it a point to remain close – partly because of the studio, but mostly because of who we are. When Richard offered me a job at the label, I found myself torn between taking it, and not abandoning Emily.

She was awesome.

After I accepted the job, I went to talk to her about it, and found her sitting in the lobby, with a box containing all the stuff from my office. When I suggested that she and Leonard buy me out, she laughed, hugged me, and said, "Until one of us dies, this will always be *our* studio, Willie…" Then, she gave me the box, and said, "Richard called and asked why you aren't in *his* studio, mixing something."

Then, she simply walked away...

While everyone in the band has tried to maintain close friendships – simply because of what we shared – Emily and I go deeper than that. She is, and I believe always will be, my best friend.

"Can you take a break, or will Richard get his underwear wadded up?"

This time, Emily cracks up.

"Like I care? You need me, I'm there. Richard knows that. What's the plan?"

"You need to meet me at my parents' house, in three days. Stan needs some help, and I pretty sure it's right up your alley. Catch is, I want it to look like you just 'turned up'."

"Me? Being devious? How completely cool is that?"

"You may need your old Strat, too. Bring it, just in case..."

"Oh yeah? Sounds like some old school headbanging is on the menu..."

"Could be. His kids are trying to cover a song – it's an old alternative club dance track, by a group called Prozzäk. He didn't say which song, but after looking at their CD, I think I know which one it is – based on how he sounded."

"Prozzäk? No kidding? I have one of their CDs. You do know what the premise for their music was, right?"

"No, I wasn't paying that much attention."

She laughs – I mean *really* laughs.

"A search for true love..."

"HA! *That* definitely makes sense. The song made him think about..."

"This is gonna be fun, Willie," Emily says, right in the middle of my sentence, "you know how much I enjoy messing with Stanley. I'm glad you invited me. I'll get hold of you once I'm there, and we can figure out how to pull this off."

"Cool," I reply, now trying not to laugh myself. "Oh, and Bailey says you have to bring Melissa."

"Crap... you remember the last time the two of them were in the same place at the same time?"

"Of course – but why should they be any different, than their parents were?"

"I'll see ya then, Willie. Take care."

"Love ya girl! Be safe! Later."

I flip the phone closed, and sit watching my daughter play with a set of drumsticks, thinking. Will Cadi be willing to get into the game? She's 6000 miles, and seven time zones away. Is the connection between the five us, still that strong?

I stand up, walk to the sliding glass door, and as I stare out at Los Angeles, mumble, "...how do I make this public? It's the only way I can actually pull this off..."

"Pull *what* off, Willie Morgan?" I hear from an all too familiar voice. I turn and find my wife standing there, arms crossed, with a questioning glare on her face.

I reach over my head, do the 'adjusting my halo' thing, then smile, and say, "Ohh... nothing dear..."

She rolls her eyes, shakes her head, then turns and goes back into the kitchen.

"Come on you two, if you want to eat," I hear, as she disappears, with Bailey hot on her heels.

nine

Catrin

"Mr. Campbell? Sorry to bother you at work, but I need some help, and Stanley is being a dweeb..."

I hear him crack up.

"Sounds like my son for sure. What can I do for you, Catrin?"

Mr. Campbell has always used my full name – which I think is kind of cool.

"I need to find Emma, and Stan is playing dumb. Do you know where she might be right now?"

"No, I honestly don't. The last letter Stan got..."

"I know... was postmarked from Torino."

"Yep. I told Stan this morning that if he didn't do something to locate her, I intended to."

"Well, the lecture you gave us, way back when, aside, I wish someone would do something – the way the two of them are behaving, is beginning to wear on my very last nerve..."

Again, he laughs, while at the same moment, my phone beeps indicating I have an incoming call. I glance at the caller ID and when I see who it is, return to Mr. Campbell.

"Mr. Campbell, I need to go – Willie is calling me. Thanks for listening, and if you do find her, *please* let me know!"

"You're first on the list, young lady. Take care – and tell Willie I said 'hey'."

"Will do. Bye."

I switch over to the incoming call.

"Willie Morgan – does your wife know you are calling other women!"

"Why, are you going to tell her?"

"Yes!" I reply, laughing, which makes him laugh.

"What's up in your life, Cadi?"

"Why?"

"Huh?"

"Why do you need to know what's up in my life?"

After a few seconds of prolonged silence, I know I'm right.

"You *are* up to something, Willie Morgan! What's going on?"

"Been to the States lately?"

"You know perfectly well I haven't been there since Emily gave birth."

"Well then, you need to stop by… and… visit with your *nieces,* I think."

"Nieces?"

"Yep. They'll be visiting their grandparents three days from tomorrow…"

"*'They'?* You have Emily involved in this, too?"

I'm certain I hear him laugh…

"And that surprises you because…?"

This time, I laugh.

"Good point."

"I'm hoping the world's best bass player will drop everything, and fly to Fort Collins, just because her favorite drummer asked her to."

"Of course I will. But will you at least tell me why I'm doing it?"

"Stan and Emma…"

"Enough said. Have you found her then?"

"*Huh?*" he blurts out.

"Well now, isn't this interesting…" I reply, with a snicker.

Willie and I spend the next forty minutes explaining to each other what we're up to. He tells me about the song that apparently got to Stan, and I tell him about my plan to get Emma to sing with the orchestra – and which song prompted me to do it. The moment he suggests 'making it public', I immediately know exactly how to do it.

All I have to do… is find Emma…

The call finished, I sit quietly, phone in hand, in the middle of my parents' living room, starting at the fire burning in the fire place, lost in thought.

The fact that *all of us* seem to have thought about finding Emma, *at the same time*, is curious, to say the least.

After a few minutes, my father comes in, and stands silently watching me.

"Catrin?" he finally says, walking over, and kneeling in front of me. "What is it, daughter?"

I smile, force myself not to laugh, and say "Fate and destiny, Tad. *Fate and destiny.*"

ten

Emily

OUTSIDE EMILY'S HOUSE, AT THE WATER'S EDGE

The day Stanley called and told me that Emma had disappeared off the face of the earth, I went off the deep end.

It happened the year after Melissa was born...

TWENTY MONTHS AGO
EMILY AND LEONARD'S HOUSE

"Emily – please! You must calm down. You're scaring Melissa!" Lenny said, as he grabbed my shoulders and made me sit down.

During my ranting, I became so distraught, and disoriented, that my husband threatened to call for outside help.

Finally, not knowing what else to do, he did call my mom. Late the next day she, and the twins, showed up, and we had a 'family thing'.

A week later, Mr. Campbell sent each of us – the remaining band members – tickets 'home', with a note attached that said attendance was *mandatory*...

The very next day, Lenny put me, along with my mom, the twins, and Melissa, on a plane to Fort Collins. He stayed behind to handle the studio.

TWENTY MONTHS AGO
THE CAMPBELL HOME

It took poor Cadi, almost forty-eight hours of traveling to get to Fort Collins, and she looked rough when she got there. She did, however, show up with the rest of us for the 'mandatory band meeting'.

None of us had the guts to point out to Mr. Campbell that the 'band' hadn't been, in well over two years...

Instead, we all sat quietly, and listened intently, as Stan's dad did his best to clarify what he felt was going on...

"Look inside yourselves – each of you. Are you content with where life has taken you?"

Starting with Cadi, he locked eyes with each of us, and held our gaze until we answered him.

"Yes sir," Cadi replied.

On to Willie...

"I am, very much so."

Then me...

I laid Melissa down on the floor in front of me, then turned, looked at him, and said, "Definitely."

Then Stanley.

When he didn't respond, Mr. Campbell actually laughed, and said, "Figures..."

Everyone saw the facial exchange between them, and knew it was something we weren't supposed to know about.

"Doesn't Emma have the right to find her way – to find some kind of contentment, even if it *doesn't* include us?"

He got us – all of us. In turn, we each answered with a mumbled 'yes'.

"If you guys turn this into some kind of bizarre spectacle by trying to hunt her down, what do you think that will do to your 'friendships'?"

"But Dad, it's as if, in her mind, we aren't friends any longer. True friends don't erase you and move on..."

"That's what your *eyes* are seeing, Stanley. Try using your *heart*..."

He paused, and stared at the drink in his hands for a few seconds.

"How can you – any of you..." he asked, making eye contact with each of us, "...truly know what is going on in Emma's head? Each of us has *'family'* – flesh and blood we are directly related to. None of you can convince me you have any idea how Emma sees the world... *every day*. Sure, we are all her family, but not in the same sense. We have brothers and sisters, aunts and uncles, husbands and wives..." he paused and glanced at Willie, then looked directly at me, "...and now, children."

We watched as he took a really deep breath, and let it out again.

"What does Emma have?"

As I sat there, totally lost in the pain we could all see in Mr. Campbell's eyes, I finally figured it out. Until that very moment, I had never actually considered that Emma could truly believe she was alone in the world. It was a case of taking my own life, totally for granted...

After a few moments of silent contemplation, Mr. Campbell made his final comment.

"I want the four of you to stop thinking about yourselves for just a bit – and try to think about Emma. Weigh this – she didn't sell the house, or her car. All her bank accounts are still open – I know because my name is on all of them. And finally, not only is her studio still completely intact, but *Gram's piano*, as well as every instrument she owns, is still down there."

We all watched him finish the 'something on the rocks' he'd been holding the entire time, set the glass down, then again look at us.

"I ask each of you, is that the behavior of someone who has abandoned her life?"

Then he turned and left the room, leaving each of us, with our own thoughts.

OUTSIDE EMILY'S HOUSE, AT THE WATER'S EDGE

Now, as I sit here watching my daughter and husband, splashing around in the crystal blue water of Lake Tahoe, I've made up my mind. It's time to get her back. One way or the other, it's time for all of us to face each other – no matter what that means. Willie's call is the driving factor.

"You have always been the big destiny person, Emma, so now yours, and ours, are about to collide…"

With a slightly devious smirk on my face, I reach down and click play on the laptop in front of me, and adjust my guitar. It's only taken me a week to cover the minimal guitar parts of the song, and I'm really not sure why I did.

It just seems like I'm… *supposed to*…

eleven
Stanley

"Thanks for walking with me, Stan…"

Courtney is beside me, holding my hand tightly.

"This is my favorite part of the day, Court – right after the sun sets, and things cool off. Spending it with you increases that exponentially."

The look in her eyes tells me something's up – I have no idea what, but something.

"It was so awesome of your dad to take us to dinner, and that restaurant is amazing."

"That's my dad…"

"I need to tell you something, Stan – that's why I wanted to walk with you…"

"Okay," I reply, smiling, "you have my undivided attention."

"I took a few extra days off, and I'm going back to Boston early."

"Okay. And?"

"No 'and'… I just wanted to tell you. I plan on staying for a couple weeks. My sister is flying in too."

"I'll go with you, if you want me to."

"Stanley, we both know you don't want to go to Boston."

When I look at her, I can see her eyes clouding up, as the moonlight reflects in them.

"What's wrong, Court?"

"Nothing. Let's just enjoy the evening, and the walk."

She looks away, but maintains her grip on my hand.

I'm pretty sure this is the exact moment that my fifth relationship goes south.

Nine hours later, I'm still awake, watching the moon move across the sliding glass door in my – I mean *our* – bedroom. Courtney's head is resting on my chest, her arm is wrapped securely around me, and she seems to be sleeping peacefully.

At 2:00 AM, on an unusually warm mountain night, while one woman sleeps on my chest, I make up my mind that I am going to find another one – and as God is my witness, she *is* going to marry me.

Let's see you avoid that bit of *destiny*, Emma Greene.

twelve
Emma

Here I sit, on the bright green grass of the Parco del Valentino, silently watching the Poe River, as it flows through Torino, Italy, on its way... somewhere.

And, as usual, I'm writing – or actually typing.

I suppose I should explain how I ended up here – close to 6000 miles from 'home'...

Eight months after our final show at CSU, I left Fort Collins, to find something. I had no idea what, but I had the most bizarre and persistent feeling that I was supposed to be somewhere other than where I was – even if I had no idea where, or why. So one afternoon, with a backpack, a credit card, and my passport, I got on a plane.

I ran away – not the way I had intended, but ran away none the less. I'd meant to just leave – no warnings, no discussions, just get up one morning and go. But, I sorta got busted in the act of sneaking off...

TWENTY TWO MONTHS AGO
EMMA'S HOUSE

I wrote a long letter to Stanley, asking him to keep an eye on the house and my car, suggesting he may want to rent the house out – if he found someone he trusted. That was my way of telling him I was going to be gone awhile. I checked carefully to make sure only the very necessary things had power, and that everything was locked. Then I called a cab to take me to airport. That's where it got complicated...

As I stepped off the porch, I saw Logan standing next to my cab, looking *very* irritated. I knew I was in trouble, the moment our eyes met.

"Why, Emma?" she asked, leaning into the cab, and handing the driver a twenty dollar bill.

"Sorry for the inconvenience, but we won't need you."

The look on her face was enough to ensure I didn't question her actions.

"Logan... I have to. Honest to God... I have to do this."

"I repeat – *why?*"

She pointed at her truck which was in the driveway, and without a word, I turned and headed toward it.

Over the years, she and I have become close to a point that can't really be explained. In my mind, Logan is, in every logical aspect, my older sister.

"There has to be more to it than this, Logan... there has to be..." I said in answer to her question, as she opened the door and waited for me to get in. She closed the door, and I watched her walk around and get in behind the wheel.

She sat there, hands on the steering wheel, staring at the front of the house – in silence. Finally, after glancing at me, she started the truck and backed out. It took less than a minute before I figured out she was taking me to the airport. When we got there, she pulled off short of the entrance and parked alongside the road.

"Emma, I'm scared – for you. No one – *none of us* – is ever going to be able to understand what it means to be you. And we both know it's not something you could ever explain. I just really need to know that you do realize you *aren't alone* – you *do* have family…"

I had to force myself to look her in the eyes…

"My heart tells me you are about to go down a dangerous path, but it also knows I can't – and shouldn't – stop you."

"Logan, I'm telling you… I'm *supposed* to do this. For the last few months, I've had the weirdest feeling that Stan too, has to go a *specific direction*."

I could see in her eyes what she wanted to say – what she wanted to say almost every time we talked.

"I can't, Logan – I just can't. Even though my heart desperately wants to, my brain keeps telling me that if we do it, all we'll do is screw up our lives."

At this point, we're both fighting our tears.

"I just need some time to figure Emma out… that's all. And, Stanley needs to travel his path."

I reached out, and gently squeezed her hand.

"Remember, the future can, and usually does, surprise us. Who knows where we'll end up?"

"Think about this, Emma – ever since Grams died, you have been running – constantly. I've never been able to figure out if it has been to, or away from something. Eventually, you'll have to stop. You know as well as I do, destiny can't be avoided…

"That's the point, Logan – I honestly believe Stan and I have to travel different paths, to get where we're going."

For just a moment, I got the strangest rush, and broke out in goose bumps.

"It's… well… *necessary.*"

Logan gave me an odd look, then put the truck in gear, and continued into the airport. A minute later, we pulled up outside the departure terminal.

"You *are* taking this," she said, pulling a gray cell phone out of her purse, "and you *will not* toss it or ignore it. When I call your sorry little butt, you *will* answer it – *every damn time. Do you understand me?*"

I let out a muffled laugh, realizing that I had the most awesome 'big sister' in the world. I put the phone and accessories, into my backpack.

"It's already set up for international use, and I will be paying the bill. It has every possible plug you could need to charge it, so you can't use 'dead battery' as an excuse. I know I can't make you use it, but for God's sake, Emma, *please don't cut us off...*"

"Who knows about it?" I asked, wiping the tears off my face.

"Me and you. If you will play my way, I give you my word, I won't tell anyone – not even your 'dad' – about it, short of some dire emergency."

I leaned over, hugged her, and said, "Fair enough. I'll keep it on during the day, and if it rings, I answer – promise."

She gently kissed my forehead and as the tears began to trickle down her cheeks, whispered "I will ask God, every day, to watch over you. Take care, Emma, and remember we're here, waiting for you..."

I got out and hurried into the airport, forcing myself not to look back. An hour and twenty-two minutes later the plane lifted off, and my adventure began – and I think I may have cried all the way to England...

BACK IN THE PARCO DEL VALENTINO TORINO, ITALY.

So, the rest of the story...

I'm not alone. A few months into my 'adventure', I acquired a 'traveling companion'.

His name is Christopher...

SIXTEEN MONTHS AGO
ON A TRAIN
SOMEWHERE BETWEEN ENGLAND AND FRANCE

Having gone back to England to straighten out some passport and visa issues, I was headed back to Europe to continue my adventure.

I was sitting alone, eyes closed, listening to *Journeys End*, when my epiphany occurred. I heard a strange series of notes – musical notes – over the music playing in my ears, which made me open my eyes.

When he came into the car, the first thought I had was, 'he looks so stressed'.

As I pulled the buds out of my ears, we made eye contact, and I smiled at him. When the doors between the cars hissed closed, I again heard the notes...

And my heart stopped...

It was as if someone put my brain on a loop, and the same notes kept playing in my head, over and over, as he walked past me, without even a nod. In the blink of an eye, my mind flashed back to a piano keyboard, in a cabin, in the New Mexico wilderness... and everything came into perfect focus.

Then, it got even stranger. When the doors cycled a second time, I looked to find a young couple had come through them – *without the musical notes playing!* There was a hiss of air, as they opened and closed, and nothing else.

Realization flooded into me.

It's him! *He's the reason I'm here!*

I dropped everything on the seat next to me, jumped up, and was about to go after him, but when

I turned around, there he was – staring at me. Still frowning, he introduced himself, and extended his hand. The moment I took it... I knew.

As I stood holding his hand and looking into his eyes, the doors opened a third time, and yes, *the same series notes from my dream*, played again...

I'd left Fort Collins, so that destiny could ensure *I'd be in this exact spot, at this exact moment...*

BACK IN THE PARCO DEL VALENTINO TORINO, ITALY

Christopher – who is three years older than me – is running away from something. His life... his family... what he believes is his destiny. He's been running six months longer than I've been searching.

I made it clear to him, the very first night we spent together in Paris – there was no room in my life for a 'significant other'. I had to figure 'me' out before I could even begin to consider an emotional relationship – with anyone.

Truth is... even after all this time, I'm still not over my first one.

The first question everyone asks – are we in love?

I'm not. I can't speak for Christopher.

The answer to the next question is yes, there is a 'physical' aspect to our relationship – sort of. It's strange in that it isn't a constant thing. It's usually spontaneous, and will go on for a while, once it starts. To see us, you would think we were in fact a 'couple'. Then, days, weeks – and once, months later, we're back to being Christopher and Emma.

Two *friends* on an adventure.

It is important to point out that 'physical' didn't begin immediately. We actually shared rooms, and beds, for almost seven months, before it happened the first time.

And, truth is, it was me who initially instigated it – not him.

I'm still struggling mentally, with all of that – and what it says about me as a person.

A lot of my confusion comes out when I write…

Anyhow, for the last year and a half, we've been living our adventure together – one day at a time. So far, it's been completely amazing.

thirteen

Catrin

Tomorrow morning, I am leaving for the States.

Right now, however, I'm sitting at a table outside 'The Café' – the same place Lenny and Emily had their 'moment' – waiting for Martha. We're going to eat, and then we're off to a jazz club to hear a new local sax player.

Because there are a lot of university students in the area, it isn't unusual to hear music – usually *loud* – as cars pass by. This time, it's a bright red BMW with its windows down. I recognize the song – *hostage* by *Ransom* – the moment I hear it, and momentarily get a rush of goose bumps.

It's the last commercial song Emma wrote, before she 'got on with her life'. That's what we decided to call what she'd done – instead of 'disappearing'. I'm not sure why, but when I first heard it, I memorized the words.

Now, although the car has passed, the lyrics are still playing in my head.

Shaking off the thought, I put in my ear buds, and am about to push play on my iPod, when I feel a hand on my shoulder.

"Hey..." I hear whispered behind me, and turn to find Martha.

"Hey," I reply, pulling the buds out, and laying the iPod on the table.

"Whatcha listening to?"

"The song from the CD... again. I'm still trying to figure out 'who' and 'why'."

"It's really bugging you, isn't it?"

"Yeah… and I don't even know why. I decided that part of my life is behind me now…"

"Oh come on, Cadi… do we – *any of us* – ever truly leave our past behind?"

I sit staring at her, thinking about what she said…

"It's okay, Cadi – you need to accept that. You guys were awesome – hell, you were actually pretty epic. All of that is still – and will always be – part of you. The Hall isn't an arena, and an orchestra isn't a pop band. Quit trying to lose yourself in *this life*, in an attempt to forget *that life*. It isn't – *as you can see* – working and it never will. You have to find space for both in your life, or you are gonna end up miserable."

I sit and stare at her for a moment, my mind racing. Then, for the first time in well over two years, my emotions actually get away from me – probably because of the 'Emma' situation. When my heart overrides my brain, and takes control of my mouth, I don't even try to stop it.

"I miss it, Marti… I *really, really*, miss it. And…" I feel my eyes begin to tear up, "*I really miss them…*"

"And… I bet if you ask your friends, you will discover, they miss it, and you, just as much," she replies, smiling at me. "Maybe…" she continues, "it's time? Your fans – *me included* – have waited a long time…"

She's interrupted when my phone, lying on the table next to my purse, starts ringing. I smile at Martha, reach out and gently squeeze her hand, then pick up the phone. When I glance at the caller ID, I recognize the country code, and the area code, but have no idea whose number it is. I flip it open and answer it.

"Catrin."

"Cadi, what's your current email address?" a female voice – that sounds somehow familiar – asks.

"Excuse me?"

"I need your email address – more importantly, *you need* what I am going to send you."

"I see. Do you make it a habit to call strangers and ask them for email addresses?"

"Oh, Catrin... you know me far better than you think. And, it's probably better you don't recognize my voice."

The moment she uses my full name, I know.

"Okay, let's say I give you the address, why do I need what you are going to send?" I reply, playing along, and resisting the urge to verify who I suspect it is.

"Two days ago you started on a quest, but were stalled. What I'm going to send you, will allow you to continue that quest..."

"popbassist2 at uk dot yahoo dot com," I blurt out, even before she finishes her sentence.

"Check it in say... ten minutes. Make sure you are at an internet capable *computer* – *not* your phone – when you do. Follow the instructions and you'll understand the 'why'..."

"Okay. And thank you."

"YOU have to finish this, Cadi... for all of us. I've done what I can."

She breaks the connection before I can respond, so I close the phone, then sit and stare blankly at Martha.

"That was a bizarrely cryptic conversation – do I want to know what it was about?"

"Fate and destiny, Marti... fate and destiny," I reply, standing up and dropping a tip on the table. "Come on, I need to find a computer."

"Sit," she replies, laughing and pulling an HP Mini out of her backpack, and putting it on the table.

"Can you get it online?"

"Yes, silly, it has a built-in air card."

I drop back into my chair, and watch as she powers it up, logs into her provider, and then spins it around so it's facing me.

"There you go. You aren't going to hack anything, are you? I don't want the police after me..." she says, a big goofy grin covering her face.

"I dunno, let's find out."

I log into my account, and find an email from someone called 'finaldestiny2020', which I open.

Inside are three lines of text:

www.worldtracking.com

A login, a password, and...

NZ876-99870-101761-COUSA.

As Martha diligently watches every keystroke, I log into the website and, once the welcome screen appears, read the instructions – which are absurdly simple.

"Type in the identifier assigned to the device you wish to track," I read out loud, and then do.

When I hit 'return', an animated icon appears with the word 'CHECKING' blinking under it. Seconds later, a small pop-up window appears with the message, 'THAT IS A VALID SYSTEM IDENTIFIER'. Just as quickly as it appeared, it disappears, and the blinking word under the animated icon changes to 'SEARCHING'. Ten seconds later, the icon disappears and a map of Italy replaces the login screen.

"oh my god..." arbitrarily comes out of my mouth.

As soon as the map finishes loading, the icon returns, and as it does its animation thing, the words 'DEVICE LOCATED – TRACKING' appear under it. Ten seconds later, the map reloads, and zooms on a specific part of Torino, Italy. One blink of an eye later, in an area labeled a park, next to a river, a blinking red 'cell phone' icon appears, with a latitude and longitude beside it.

I burst into tears the moment I read the caption under it: 'Little Sister'

My heart races as I realize that it *was Logan* on the phone. More importantly, she's just given me the means to find Emma.

Then, in the midst of the tension, and euphoria, a thought pops into my head, which I inadvertently verbalize…

"Apparently, Logan has known all along, where Emma is…"

Tears now freely trickling down my cheeks, I pull out my phone and dial. He answers on the first ring.

"Willie… it's me. Something's come up and I'm gonna have to postpone coming…"

fourteen
Emma

"Okay, Miss Greene, you ready to go eat?"

Christopher, who just walked up, is holding out his hand to me.

"Did you talk to your boss?" I ask, letting him pull me to my feet.

"I did. He understands, but isn't happy that I quit. What about you?"

"I told Gina we were leaving," I reply, locking my fingers through his, as we cross the park, headed for our favorite café. "She's sad, but understands I think."

"I told the landlord we'll be gone in a week. He said we were wonderful tenants, and he hopes we will seek him out if we come back."

"Not likely," I reply, kissing Christopher on the cheek.

It's time to move on – to continue on our path. To see where it leads. A new place, new acquaintances, and new jobs. A new life. We take turns deciding when to go, and where to go. In the last eighteen months, we've lived – however briefly – in six different towns, in four different countries. I honestly believe that everyone should do this – for at least a little while – to gain a better understanding of the world around us.

"I guess I'm picking this time, right?"

"Uh-huh," I reply, leaning over and gently biting his earlobe.

He smiles at me, makes a quick turn, and five minutes later, we're home – instead of at dinner.

We've slipped into one of our 'amorous' periods, and for the last week, all I seem think about is him – and being in contact with him. At times, I'd almost believe that Christopher and I are quite possibly, the two most *physically* compatible people on the entire planet, as bad as that may sound.

Our seemingly perfect compatibility leads to an ongoing question I've been asking God... *'How can two people be so totally compatible, and yet not be in love?'*

And, of course, I keep answering the question...

'Because I am, and always have been, completely lost in the very first love of my life.'

That being said, why in the world am I still here, with Christopher? Why haven't I gone back to the only man I've ever been in love with?

What am I so damn afraid of?

Just one, of many examples, showing how totally screwed up, Emma's head actually is.

As I lay here, completely exhausted, my head resting on Christopher's chest, the rhythmic beating of his heart filling my mind, my thoughts are actually elsewhere – still locked into a looping playback, of a strange and bizarre sensation, that rushed through me earlier, at the park.

Something is about to change... I can feel it.

Something other than us moving on...

fifteen
Stanley

"Georgia – would you do your brother a favor?"

"Of course. Whacha need?" Georgia replies.

My little sister – who is now actually sixteen, and not all that 'little' anymore – is at the house to sort some school papers, and enter some grades into the school computer for me, just as she does every Thursday afternoon. In addition to being 'grown up', she's also outgrown her nickname, and prefers to be called by her given name – which I think is awesome.

"Call this guy," I hand her a yellow sticky I'm holding, "and tell him I need to talk to him about one of his old songs. If you get a secretary or something, use Emily's studio or the band's name to get through. Be your tricky, sneaky little self, and get me five minutes to talk to him."

"I'm on it."

She takes the slip of paper, walks over, sits down at my desk, and picks up the phone.

"Hey," I hear from behind me, and feel a pair of arms wrap around my waist.

I spin around, and gently kiss Courtney.

"Hey babe."

"Can I borrow you, while your admin assistant hustles people for you?"

"I heard that!" Georgia yells, making us laugh.

"Sure. Front steps? Or..." I whisper, glancing at my sister, "did you have something else in mind?"

"Although tempting, the front steps would be more appropriate."

I follow her down the hall, onto the porch, and then sit down beside her on the steps.

"I'm not coming back, Stanley."

"*Huh?*"

"Here..." she says, holding out her keys, "...and thank you. Maybe your dad will let you give the car to Georgia."

She caught me so completely off guard, that for the first time in as long as I can remember, I'm truly speechless. After a second, she continues.

"Oh come on, Stanley. You can't tell me you weren't expecting this."

"Just like that? What's going on Court?"

"It's time for *both of us* to be honest. Neither of us really wants to keep doing this..."

It's as if she reached in, and grabbed my heart. I'm pretty sure my facial expression, the moment she says it, totally gives me away. After a few seconds, she reaches over and takes my hands.

"Look... back when we started this, I told you about my past, and how I ended up here. You know that I ran away, and why. I was young, Stanley, and didn't know what else to do.

"When you found me, I was a mess, but the first time you touched me, my heart relaxed and my problems seemed to fade. You took a huge chance, when you gave me a chance. A *week* after you met me, you took me to Paris – *for no particular reason.* Who does that for someone they just met, Stanley?

"You – *and your family* – welcomed me with open arms, and made me feel like I belong. For that I will be eternally grateful to all of you.

"But... well... I have to find out for sure, Stan."

All I can do is watch, as the tears slowly begin to trickle down her cheeks.

"When I get there, I intend to try to find him. My sister is going to help me. Thing is, my heart won't let me do that without telling you first.

"I have no idea what might have become of me, if it had been anyone other than you, that found me, Stanley. You have become the single most important person in the last year and a half of my life, and I wouldn't change any of it.

"But I need to know. I need to see him... to have him tell me if we can recover after all this time. Once he does that, I'll accept whatever answer he gives me, and move on. Not knowing, is worse than knowing I've lost him."

She pauses for a second, as if trying to decide how to continue.

"My heart keeps telling me that it would be totally unfair to leave you here, thinking that I'm coming back... because I know perfectly well, that's not going to happen."

"I know Courtney... I know. I do believe we love each other, but in all fairness, neither of us is *in love* with the other."

"I suspected you might feel that way..."

She looks down at our hands, and sits silently for a moment.

"Sometimes..." she finally says, lifting her head and looking at me, "when you are looking at me, your eyes tell me you're seeing her – seeing Emma."

I feel myself blush, the moment she says it.

"It's been more pronounced for about the last six months. And of course, there are the lyrics..."

"You've read them?"

"Yes. You tend to leave them lying around, and I figured..."

"And you're right. If I didn't want you reading them I'd have put them away. Emma has always had a way with words... with verse. And even though at times, one has to concentrate, she always seems to be able to convey her message."

"Are *you* getting the message, Stanley? You two need to quit torturing yourselves – and everyone else in your lives as well – and concede that it's your destiny to be together. Everyone else can see it Stan, why can't the two of you?"

We hear the squeak at the same moment, and turn to find my sister standing in the doorway, sad-faced, staring at us.

Georgia lets go of the screen door, takes a step down, pushes in between us, and sits down. She turns and faces Courtney first.

"My brother has managed to date two totally awesome girls in his life – you're the second of the two. I've gotten really attached to you, Courtney, and no matter what happens here and now, I honestly hope that as I get older, and find my way in the world, you will still be there – as my friend and big sister."

Courtney finally smiles, wipes her tears, and hugs Georgia. Then, my little sister turns to face me.

"Stanley Campbell – you are my big brother, and the closest person to me in the entire world. But, for the last three years, you and my other 'big sister' have been behaving like a couple of big dweebs. Courtney is totally right on this one. Will you *please* quit screwing around and do what needs to be done?"

She leans over, kisses my cheek, then stands up and heads back into the house, pausing at the door.

"And... Mr. Levine – who made the comment, *'Stan Campbell? Wasn't he in a band called...'* to which I replied, 'yes he was' – told me to have you call him anytime about his songs. He said his secretary would put you through, no questions asked. I left the number he gave me on your desk. I'm going to the gym – see you guys later."

"Hey!" I yell after her, as the screen slams, "How'd you pull that off?"

"Easy!" she yells back. After a few seconds she reappears, backpack over her shoulder, arms full of books, and again steps between us. She's halfway to Emma's Jeep Cherokee, which is parked at the curb, when she answers my question – over her shoulder, without looking back.

"He thinks I'm *Audio Distortion's* producer..."

Courtney and I break up laughing as we watch her get into the Jeep, start it, and then disappear down the street.

Our last night together is a quiet, solemn one. Courtney falls asleep with her head on my chest – for the last time. And... for the first time in months, I too, fall soundly asleep.

The next day, I stand quietly and watch, as Courtney passes through the security checkpoint at the airport, and then disappears into the crowd, without looking back.

As strange as it will sound, I have a bizarre feeling that, even as short as it was, her presence in my life, was... well... *planned.*

As Emma would say... *it was supposed to happen – exactly the way it did.*

sixteen

Catrin

"You look *beautiful*, Catrin. How you go from jeans to *this*, fascinates me, each time you do it.

"Oh, Tad..." I reply, using the Welsh word for father, as I always do. Although I do speak our native tongue, I'm not what you would consider fluent, unfortunately.

"If I can make you smile, it's worth it," I add, squeezing his hand.

I'm pretty sure it's more about the red hair, freckles, and bright green eyes, than what I am wearing, but my mum is really good about dressing me (yeah, I'm kinda lazy when it comes to clothes) in stuff that accents me.

But... my father is right – get me out of the jeans, and into a dress, and I get noticed.

A lot.

Even on an airplane.

Guys my age, older men, even young kids – *of all ethnicities* – seem drawn to me when I dress up – more so, when a lot of me is showing. Like today.

I'm wearing a jet-black (my mum has this thing about black...) silk and mesh, halter dress, that's covered with brilliant red embroidery, and accents, and goes all the way to the floor. It's completely backless, fits quite tightly above the waist, and opens up at the bottom.

My friends were kinda shocked when they discovered *my mother* picked it out, and then, my father actually agreed to buy it. And yes... it did take me a while to get comfortable with the whole 'attention' thing.

"And thank you, Tad, from the deepest part of me, for coming. Your strength will help me."

"Remember when you last went in search of your friends?"

"I do."

"Although I was hesitant, from that experience I learned that some things simply must be done – without explanation. Emma needs you, and so, you must go."

I lean forward as my father puts a shawl over my bare shoulders, and then wraps it around me. I smile at him, then reach down and smooth the wrinkles from my dress.

We land in Torino just after 7:00 PM, take a taxi to a very nice hotel my father made reservations at, and check in. When he suggests two rooms, I laugh and tell the clerk that one room, with two beds, will be fine.

As the clerk completes her paperwork, I turn to face my father.

"I'm not so old, that I can't still share a room with my father."

My father and the clerk laugh. She hands us our key cards, then looks directly at me.

"Miss Meredith – that is the most beautiful dress I have seen in a very long time. I cannot imagine it could be so beautiful on anyone else..."

Yeah... she makes me blush. Instantly.

Once we make it to the room, I get into my sweats (*finally!*) and then sit crossed-legged on the bed, Martha's laptop in front of me, staring at the screen. After a few moments, my father comes and sits next to me.

"Such deep thought, daughter. I will listen, if you wish to talk."

"I'm wondering if what I'm about to do, is a good thing."

"What do you mean?"

"Why am I doing it – to help Emma, or is it just selfish intent? If she wanted contact with us…"

"Perhaps, Cadi, she only needs a nudge – just as she did, all those years ago."

When I look at him, the warm smile on his face puts me at ease. I log in, and once again, try to find my missing friend.

This time, instead of finding Emma's phone, I get a message telling me the phone is apparently turned off. The system does, however, give me 'the last known location of the device' – which, after I use the system to locate my computer, turns out to be less than two miles from me.

Sleep, I know, is going to be impossible.

seventeen
Emma

Because Christopher agreed to finish out the week, he got up this morning, and went to work at the small computer shop, in the downtown area, that took a chance and hired him seven weeks earlier. Part of the deal that had been struck, was that Christopher would help the owner, Alberto, and his son Matteo, with their English. It's something Christopher truly enjoys, and thrusts himself into completely. On occasion, I stop by and get into it as well, mostly because the vigor the two of them exhibit, while walking round repeating things in English, truly astounds me. *They really want to learn English.*

My job at a small, local café has always been more of a 'mercy assist', than a real job. When I explain to Gina what's going on, she tells me that I should spend my time planning our trip, and that she'll be fine. She also gives me her address and phone number, telling me that no matter where my journey takes me, she hopes I will find time to stay in touch with her. When she hugs me for the last time, she says, "Friends made in Italy, become family, and last until time ends."

Having five hours to kill, I am once again sitting on the grass in the park, writing – this time, lyrics generated by listening to my 'phantom CD'. It's as if something inside, is driving me to compose them, so I simply let my mind and fingers go…

The moment the pocket of my sweater starts ringing, I smile and pull out the gray, rubberized phone I've carried with me every day, for the last twenty-two months.

"Hey, Logan!"

"Hey little sister. You ready to come home yet?"

"No, Sis... not quite yet. Soon, though."

"I still miss you."

"Back atcha."

"Everything's good in your world?"

"It is..."

"Well... be safe and think about me."

"Every day, Logan... every day."

"Love you girl. Talk to you soon. Bye."

"Bye..."

Just like I do each time she calls, I force back the tears, close the phone, and put it back in my pocket.

We've had that exact same conversation fifty-one times in the last two years – and yes, I have been counting.

Logan didn't call me at all during the first four months I was gone. I think that she was hoping I'd get home sick, turn around, and go back. When that didn't happen, the calls started.

At first, she did her best to talk me into going back, and when that didn't work, she took to calling twice a day hoping, I think, to 'interrupt' something, or perhaps, get someone else to answer the phone.

After seven months of silliness, we finally had to actually talk.

I told her she had to accept what I was doing, and that until I sorted out my heart, I couldn't come 'home'. At one point, although I wouldn't have really done it, I threatened to mail the phone back to her.

I think that was her breaking point – the point at which she conceded defeat. She apologized, crying the entire time. I told her that she was my anchor, and that I wanted to hear from her – but that she had to stop using our communication as a means of coercion.

She didn't call again for two weeks – which, at the time, did freak me out a bit. The day before she did call, I was actually considering calling her. We finally agreed that she would call every other week – on a day of her choosing – just to check on me. If I wanted to talk, good, if not, we'd keep it short.

What I do find amusing, is that she always seems to know when it's day where I am – although I've never once told her where I am, nor has she asked. She's never once called after the sun has set – no matter what time zone I'm in.

I know that I owe Logan – big time. It's because of her concern for me, that I still have a 'home' – a place to return to, when I'm ready.

As words flow from my head to my keyboard, 'the song' is playing in my ears for hundredth time in the last week. I backspace, change this, move that, and then start the process again. I continue what can sometimes become a tense emotional battle, and eventually my thoughts drift to Stanley... and all the random stuff I've sent him over the last two years.

Why you ask, have I kept sending him lyrics? I've spent hours considering that very same question...

And... I'm pretty sure we know the answer.

Anyhow, I know Stanley has been writing for a bunch of new artists since I left, and I figure Richard probably keeps him pretty busy with his upstarts as well. At one point I saw an interview with the group 'Hot Chelle Rae', and they mentioned that Stan wrote one of the songs on their new album, and co-wrote another.

The one absolute constant in the entire universe that I'm certain of is, Stanley Campbell and music, will be eternally synonymous. And, if you think about it, that probably applies to me as well. No matter where I am, who I am with, or what I may be doing, I write – constantly. I even have a *full*, 300-page notebook, to prove it.

I have no idea what – other than fate and destiny – makes me raise my head when I do, but the moment I see her, my heart stops. Not because she's here – *in Italy* – but because of how *utterly amazing* she looks.

She's wearing the most beautiful jet-black dress I have ever seen. Her shiny, bright red hair – which is *much* longer than I remember it – is hanging loosely around her shoulders, and is being gently blown by the wind, as she crosses the park at a moderate pace, headed *directly for me*.

Around her neck is a silver and onyx choker that matches her earrings, and the bangles on her wrists. This is far past anything she ever wore when the band...

I feel myself choking up, and quickly let the thought fade.

When I glance around, I realize that every single head she passes turns, and watches her, not looking away until she finally stops directly in front of me.

Completely speechless, at this point, I watch as she carefully lifts her dress, so she will have room to move, and then kneels down on the grass, directly opposite me.

Truth is... I simply can't remember ever seeing *anything* as beautiful as Catrin Meredith is, at this exact moment.

"Fy mod wedi colli eich, Emma," she says, in Welsh so perfect, you'd think it's her first language.

When I sit silent, and motionless – still in a state of shock – for a few seconds, she leans over, gently kisses my cheek, and says, "I've missed you, Emma."

I burst full-on into tears. The deep sobbing kind.

It takes over thirty minutes, and the constant consoling of Mr. Meredith – who appears out of nowhere – to bring my emotions back under control.

eighteen

Emma

We – Cadi, Mr. Meredith and I – are sitting at a sidewalk table, at Christopher's favorite café. I've been meeting him here each afternoon, and we walk home together.

Yes, I'm scared. Actually, petrified is a better word – which becomes blatantly evident, as I reach down, and pick up my coffee. The moment Cadi sees how badly my hand is shaking, she reaches over, takes my free hand and gives it a gentle squeeze. I take a sip of coffee, and give her a forced smile.

The two parts of my life that I've managed to keep separate for a year and a half, are about to collide, and there is no way to stop it.

I'm only half-listening to Cadi tell me about her plan to have me sing with their orchestra, when Christopher appears up the street from us. The moment I put the cup down, Cadi notices the change in my demeanor and she looks up the street, and at the same time, again gently squeezes my hand.

"It's okay, Emma. *Ymlaciwch.*"

"*Huh?*" I reply, turning to look at her. She of course, laughs.

"Catrin is right... you need to *relax*," Mr. Meredith offers, smiling, and placing his hand over both of ours. "We're not here to interfere or judge, only to recover something that has been missing from our lives, for far too long."

I try to relax, but they know the smile I give them is both nervous, and very forced. I stand up as

Christopher approaches us, and Mr. Meredith stands too, introducing himself, and shaking Christopher's hand, even before I say anything.

It's awkward – for both of us – but Christopher handles it well.

I start to kiss Christopher, and when he hesitates, opting not to kiss me, Mr. Meredith is all over it.

"Your behavior is making us feel unwelcome," he says, glaring directly at me. "You two are more than friends – any person with common sense can see this in your eyes. Do not embarrass yourselves, as well as us, by acting otherwise."

Cadi immediately stands up, and kisses her father on the cheek.

"You're the most awesome man I know, Dad."

I feel the tears coming, because none of them – meaning the band – has ever seen me with anyone other than Stanley. But, I do kiss Christopher – just as passionately as I ever have.

Once we escape the moment's awkwardness, Christopher turns, and to my complete surprise, stands silently staring at Cadi – for long enough that, because of her fair complexion, Cadi begins to blush.

"Mr. Meredith – it is not my intention to offend you," Christopher says, never taking his eyes off Cadi, who is now blushing rather badly, "but your daughter, *is the most beautiful woman I have ever seen...*"

"*oh my god...*" Cadi mutters, as a new wave of embarrassment sweeps over her, and she turns the coolest shade of red – *everywhere*.

I watch, smiling, as Christopher takes her hand, ever so gently kisses it, and then lets it go. The really intriguing thing about the whole situation is, *not once* in eighteen months, has Christopher *ever* given another female, more than a cursory glance.

"Catrin... it is my belief that the men of the world will suffer a great loss, when one is lucky enough to capture your heart."

Cadi looks as if she is gonna faint – I swear. Her dad sees it as well and quickly rescues her.

"Please, Christopher, sit and let us learn about each other. I am quite curious, to say the least, about the man who has so enthralled our Emma."

We sit drinking coffee, and talking, well into the evening, and amazingly, what I feared would turn into a disaster, is anything but.

Christopher, blatantly enthusiastic about finally being allowed into the 'secret' part of my life, opens up. Cadi and her father are excited about simply having found me.

But, as is usually the case, along with the positive, there usually comes a negative. I somehow know this is the beginning of the end for Christopher and me. The look in his eyes a number of times during the afternoon tells me he too, realizes it. It has so far been, just he and I – in the present. Now that *my* past has caught up with us, that's over.

What I find reassuring, is that Christopher's body language tells me it's okay... that *we* will be okay.

Once we get back to the apartment, the changes begin almost immediately. The previous two weeks of amorous silliness in our bedroom, ends abruptly that night. We go back to being Christopher and Emma – two *friends* who, it seems, realize that their amazing adventure is about to come to an end...

nineteen

Stanley

I'm sitting at my Roland, at the back of the stage, playing with some effects, when Pete walks up behind me.

"What's that, Mr. Campbell? Sounds familiar..."

"It's the background from that CD they delivered in class. I've been trying to figure out how they created it."

"Can I try something?" he asks.

"Always..."

I watch, as he feeds it through a digital mixer in a computer next to us, and then start clicking things. After thirty seconds, he laughs and looks at me.

"It's a voice, Mr. Campbell – they ran a voice through a synthesizer."

"And when did you get so smart?"

"I dunno... I'm always messing with stuff on my computer..."

"Let me hear it unscrambled..."

He clicks a few things, and we hear a female voice through the speakers stacked at the back of the stage. At the same time, Patty and Melinda appear behind us.

"Her pitch is a bit off," Melinda says, making the other kids laugh.

I'm right at the point of laughing myself, when an odd clicking sound fills the auditorium, and quickly becomes a repeating rhythm. Pete reaches over, shuts off the music, and we turn in unison, to find the source of the sound, only to discover a grinning

Willie Morgan, drumsticks ticking away, walking down the aisle toward the stage.

As my mind flashes back to a pizza parlor, years ago, I cross the stage to the grand piano, sit down, and jump right into the song – *the very first song we actually wrote as a band*...

Patty, now standing next to the practice drum set, recognizes the song and, as the excitement of the moment sweeps over her, glances at me. In the time it takes me to laugh and nod, the percussion part of the song fills the hall. It takes less than a heartbeat, for Melinda to join us as well.

And no, I'm not surprised – fact is, the kids can actually play almost all of *Audio Distortion*'s songs.

"Oh yeah!" Willie yells, as he climbs the steps of the stage. *"Go for it!"*

Smiling, I glance back up the aisle, and see a *very pregnant* Vicki – who has the goofiest grin on her face – sitting down in one of the seats, and Bailey in the aisle next to her, already dancing away with a couple of students.

Willie picks up a bass guitar from a stand, and does his best to fake the bass line – which makes me laugh. I nod at Pete, who has been patiently waiting, and using my Roland, he picks up the keyboards. I in turn, sit listening, and watching as the four of them crank out *Being Noticed*...

It's actually kind of amazing, and you can tell by their faces, the kids too, are caught up in the moment. Within seconds, all the kids present are clapping to the beat, and urging them on.

I slide the stool back a bit, and am about to stand up, when without warning, I'm completely blown away, by an *incredible* unamplified voice that fills the Hall – at the exact point in the song when it should...

*On a quiet night
I was cleaning tables
Watching the band
Knowing they're able*

All the clapping stops, the kids dancing suddenly stop moving, and every single head in the room turns in the direction of voice.

I too, find my head following the amazing sound, only to find Sally Wright – a freshman who has shown an interest in music – sitting at the edge of the stage, feet dangling, swaying back and forth – *and singing.* Until this exact moment, I had absolutely *no clue…*

The kids on stage never miss a beat as Sally sits, eyes closed, her feet keeping time to the music, and belts out *Being Noticed* as if was written for her. I get goose bumps, *and* have a serious flashback…

Patty and Melinda – who usually do the vocals – quickly fall in, and start singing back-up without any prompting. When I catch them grinning at each other, I begin to wonder.

I turn my attention back to Sally, realizing that I am listening to what has to be, short of Emma, the purest, most unfettered voice I have ever heard. And considering her lack of any kind of formal training, her pitch control is frighteningly perfect.

Like Emma, she is apparently a natural vocalist…

When I turn, and glance at Willie, standing behind me, he immediately raises his eyebrows and gives me a 'can you believe it?' look.

I continue toward the front of the stage, as a number of other kids start to crowd around our new vocalist. I quickly wave at them, and put a finger to my lips, hoping to keep them from spooking Sally, who is already into the second stanza. The kids, understanding my signal, stop short, and all start dancing – which is, of course, the usual response whenever a real song is played in the Hall. By the time the kids on stage make it to the final stanza, at least twenty-five other kids, have filtered in, and are dancing and singing, everywhere.

I'm fairly certain this is going to warrant a 'chewing out' from the principle – again. Rule is – NO impromptu 'concerts'. But, hearing this little girl's voice, I know it just doesn't matter.

The kids play through to the end of the song, and when I turn and look behind me, I catch Melinda high-fiving Pete, and see they both have huge grins on their faces. The moment the last note fades, the Hall erupts in cheering, clapping, and whistling.

Laughing myself, I quickly take the few steps to where Sally is sitting with her eyes closed, and sit down next to her.

"Do that very often, Sally?"

"Huh?" she replies, visibly embarrassed and blushing badly. After a second, she opens her eyes, looks first at the group of kids standing in front of her, then turns and looks at me.

"Breaking out in song – do you do it very often?"

"Not usually..." she replies, in barely a whisper. "I get embarrassed easily. I just *really* like that song..."

As we are talking, Vicki walks up, with Bailey right next to her.

"You sing really good!" Bailey blurts out, following it with a giggle.

Sally smiles at her, and again blushes – badly.

"Embarrassed? *Why?*" Vicki asks, stepping over and putting a hand on Sally's leg. "You have an *unbelievable* voice, Sally. That's nothing to be embarrassed about."

Vicki's comment is quickly followed by a number of 'totally's' and some 'no doubt's' and even a couple of '*SERIOUSLY!*'s' from the students around her.

"Thank you..." Sally mumbles, still visibly embarrassed.

"You do remember *Audio Distortion*, right?"

Sally grins at Vicki, then turns and immediately looks up at me.

"Well, yeah... everyone does."

"Well," Vicki continues, "the very first time Emma sang in front of people – by total accident – Stan and the others had to talk her out of a storage room right after it happened. She had the same problem..."

All the kids standing around break up laughing, and Willie and I join in as well.

"Thing is..." Victoria continues, "...her band mates made her understand that she has a gift – the same gift you apparently have. You just filled this place with an amazingly beautiful sound, and you did it without any help – no microphone, no electronics... *nothing*.

Vicki pauses, and purposely waits until Sally looks right at her.

"Just your voice."

Patty, Melinda and Pete walk up and stop within feet of us, and stand quietly listening.

"Sally..." I carefully put a hand on her shoulder, "if you decide to pursue music, I'm here, and would be more than honored to work with you."

She raises her head and looks at me.

"But remember this. It has to be something *Sally* wants to do. Don't let *anyone* pressure you into it."

"Thanks, Mr. Campbell. I'll think about it. But right now, I need to get home..."

As she slides off the stage, Vicki takes her hand and helps her. She heads for the exit, getting compliments from other students, the entire way. The moment the door clicks shut, I turn to face the kids on stage.

"And you didn't tell me about Sally because...?"

The three of them stand staring at me, looking seriously guilty. When Willie starts laughing, it breaks the moment.

"You saw how embarrassed she got, Mr. Campbell," Patty says.

"Yeah," Melinda adds, "it took her most of the school year to even sing in front of us, in Pete's garage..."

We stand staring at each other for few seconds, and a realization hits me – *they're just trying to protect Sally...*

"We asked her a bunch of times to sing with the band, Mr. Campbell, but she always freaks out – so we decided to let it go," Pete finally says. "She hangs around a lot when we practice, and if she sings we let her, and don't make a big deal out of it."

"That," Patty says, pointing at the spot Sally had been sitting, "was the first time since we've known her that she actually sang *in front of people*."

Now grinning, I step over and give each of them a 'fist-bump'.

"Nicely done guys... very nicely done!"

"So...," Willie says from behind me, "I hear you three have a blazing fast song you want to cover."

"Uh... well..." Pete mumbles.

I have to fight off a laugh, when I glance at Melinda and Patty, standing there, totally zoned.

"You guys want some help?"

They look right at me – instantly.

"No way – don't look at me guys. This is between you and him. I'm just the teacher…"

"We're having trouble with the tempo, Mr. Morgan," Patty finally forces out.

"Well, let's hear this song and see what we can do."

The kids turn toward the back of the stage, and are headed for the computer we were using earlier, when I stop them.

"The mp3 is on the Roland, Pete…"

They alter their course, stopping next to the keyboard, and once Pete pushes some buttons, the song begins to play through the stage speakers. Willie listens to the entire song once through, then he and the kids exchange some words, and Pete plays it again.

About half the kids in the Hall migrate down, take seats in the front row, and sit quietly watching, and listening.

After the third time through, and a brief discussion involving the sheet music, the three of them give it a try, with Willie on bass. When Patty makes a couple of mistakes, and loses herself to frustration, Willie puts the bass back in its stand, walks over, and holds out his hand to her.

"May I?"

"*OMG!* Are you kidding?" Patty replies, jumping up off her stool so quickly, she almost knocks it over.

"You *can* do this, Patty," Willie says, as she hands him her drumsticks. "Stand right here, and pay attention. Your problem isn't tempo – it's just a standard 4/4. Your problem is catching the shifts." He looks at Pete and Melinda, and says, "Shall we?"

Pete pushes a button, the song starts again, and Willie jumps right into it, immediately followed by Pete, and then Melinda.

Ten seconds later, I'm the first one to realize there's a bass line – and yet, *there is no bass player*. Although their confusion is evident, the kids keep right on playing. Willie, however, has the goofiest smirk on his face, which prompts me to look back up the aisle at Vicki. The fact I now see *two* little girls dancing in the aisle, pretty much gives away what's going on...

"*You're a lead guitarist!*" I yell over the music, following it with a laugh.

"*I'm versatile, Stanley...*" we hear Emily yell back, as she appears from behind the stage curtain, a bass guitar hanging from her shoulders, grinning.

"Step it up, Melinda... one beat..." she says, stopping right next to her.

Needless to say, Melinda is zoning at this point.

At the first break, Willie hands Patty the sticks he has in his pocket, and watching him closely, she starts playing along in the air, next to him.

"Pick up another beat, Mindy – we're close..." Emily says. Then she turns and looks at Pete, who honestly looks as if he is going to faint at any second.

"I know you're a guy, but try to keep up, Pete..." she says, making him blush, and the girls giggle. He does, however, immediately match their tempo.

"One more beat, Willie – I'm feeling it!" Emily orders, just before the third chorus.

The kids match him, and at this point, they're in sync with the recording. I'm so amazed, all I can do is smile.

Then suddenly, Emily stops them, and in her usual style, simply takes over.

"Hold on! Everyone stop. Pete, start it over. Stanley, this time use the mixer to drop each of our instruments from the track, one at time."

"You got it, Em," I reply, moving to the mixing board.

At this point, we have a crowd in excess of thirty – almost all of whom are music students – crowded up to the front of the stage. Since I started teaching, this is the very first time a 'band' is getting 'on the job training' while the students get to watch. I find myself wondering why I've never done it before.

Pete skips the intro, and the four of them jump back in when the music starts. At the break between the first chorus, and second stanza, Willie stands up, and gives Patty back her seat.

It always amazes me what a little 'direction' can do when frustration sets in. In a matter of thirty minutes, Emily and Willie taught three kids, how to overcome their issue.

Oh, and... Patty *nails* it. She's catches each shift perfectly, and is so synced, that the rest of them are now keeping time off her rhythms.

One at a time, using the mixer, I drop each instrument from the track they are playing over, and by the last stanza, it's all the kids – and Emily. By the third pass, they're totally shredding it – without playing over the track.

Once they finish, all the kids start cheering, whistling, and applauding. Willie, Emily, and I, are headed down the stairs, when we hear the kids behind us, discussing what they're going to do about the song's vocals, which makes Willie and Emily laugh.

Halfway to where Vicki is sitting, I catch a glimpse of Mrs. Marshall – our principle – standing in the main entrance, watching.

"I'll be back in a sec, guys – it's 'butt chewing' time…"

I leave them standing next to Vicki and the kids, and go to talk to the principle.

"I know the rules, Mrs. Marshall…" I start to say, just before she cuts me off.

"What I just saw wasn't an impromptu 'jam session' – it was what teaching is all about, Mr. Campbell. You had thirty *high school* kids, quietly and diligently watching what you and your friends were trying to *teach* the kids on the stage. At times, your 'technique' tends to mystify me, but you always seem to get the job done…"

She pauses, and glances in the direction of the stage, where a group of kids is still talking about the song, and going over the sheet music.

"I swear, Stanley – if you even *think* about quitting this job, I *will* hunt you down…"

Then, with a smile, she turns and walks away. Seconds later, as I am standing there shaking my head, the others join me.

"That was weird…"

"What happened?" Emily asks, picking up her daughter.

"Nothing really, but it's possible the principle may offer you and Willie jobs…" I say in response to Emily.

Being totally confused, everyone cracks up.

"So… back to my place?"

Everyone nods their agreement, and forty minutes later, we're all sitting around my living room, and I have the two cutest girls in the entire world, sitting on my lap.

twenty
Emma

"So, do you want to do it, Emma?"

"We were leaving anyhow, right?" Christopher interjects.

We're sitting in a restaurant, next door to Cadi's hotel. Her father opted to let us work out our issues on our own. Cadi insisted I bring Christopher, because he too, is invested in the situation.

"Cadi," I reply, looking across the table at her, "I haven't sung – *at all* – for close to three years. I sorta decided that part of my life is over."

A strange look momentarily washes over Cadi's face.

"Emma, I tried the same thing, just the other day. Martha made me see what I was really doing..."

"Huh? Tried what? And who's Martha?"

"Martha is my best friend actually, and her comment on the whole 'leaving the past behind' thing was, *'You need to quit trying to lose yourself in this'* – meaning my life with the orchestra – *'in an attempt to forget that'* – meaning the band."

Cadi pauses for second, and when she looks at Christopher, I see the wink he gives her.

"She also pointed out that I had to *'find space for both in my life, or I'm gonna end up miserable.'*"

I quickly realize where she's going... and why.

"God made you a *singer*, Emma. Whether you sing or not, *you are always going to be a singer.*"

She reaches across the table and takes hold of my hand, giving me a devious smirk as she does.

"And, I dare you – here and now – to look me in the eyes and tell me *you don't miss it.*"

When I don't respond, Christopher stifles a snicker, and when Cadi turns to look at him, they exchange a high-five.

"Through every single disaster each of us has faced over the years, you were always there, Emma, with 'fate and destiny' – and all of us learned to accept that. Sorry girl, but this time, I fully intend to apply them to Emma Greene."

This time Christopher can't stop his laugh.

"*YOU*, totally rock, Cadi!"

Still grinning, Christopher turns, and looks at me.

"We can spend some time back in England, and then figure things out from there. I've never been to Southport – could be interesting. And besides," he offers, a slightly devious grin spreading across his face, "since the day I finally got you to admit who you are, I've wanted to hear you sing. This," he adds, reaching out and touching my cheek, "could be the only chance I ever get…"

It's absurdly simple to figure out what he's doing. By getting me into Cadi's backyard, he'll be able to get away, without feeling he abandoned me. This is the exact moment I accept that our adventure *is going to end*.

I look at him, then at Cadi, and my heart – for some insanely bizarre reason – for just a moment, takes me back to that night in Papa Roni's, when the four of them stood in the kitchen and convinced me *we could actually be a band…*

I laugh, and say, "Okay, okay, I'll do it."

Cadi and Christopher both yell out, and again high-five each other, as I sit laughing.

The next day, Cadi and her dad head home.

Three days after that, Christopher and I land at the airport in Birmingham, and Cadi picks us up.

By then, things between Christopher and I, are slipping so quickly, I begin to worry that I'll wake up one morning, and he'll simply be gone.

twenty-one
Emma

For three days, I've been exercising my voice. People seem to find it amusing when they see me walking down the street, singing – for no apparent reason – a moveable scale, just to be sure I can hit all the notes.

The day after we got here, I was sitting alone, on the curb at a small intersection, near the auditorium, when I heard one of *Ransom*'s songs, playing on some external speakers outside a book store. It only took a second, before I picked up the vocals – to the complete surprise of more than one passing local resident.

The very next day, the inevitable occurred. Someone recognized me.

I was sitting on the grass in front of a church, reading and singing, when two teenage girls walking down the sidewalk stopped, glanced at me, then turned and whispered to each other. After a moment of hesitation, they crossed the grass, and stopped right in front of me.

"Excuse me, Miss," the first girl said, "but aren't you Emma Greene?"

"I am."

"Like… the *Audio Distortion* Emma Greene?" the second one asked.

I couldn't help it… I laughed.

"One and the same."

They instantly dropped to the grass, and within seconds, we were well into a round of 'twenty questions'. Truth is... it was actually kind of a rush, and made me think back to Cadi's challenge, at that table in Torino.

That same afternoon, the orchestra members – who are easily the most sincere group of musicians I have ever met – all but pleaded with me to sing one of the band's songs, and I happily agreed. Using her laptop, Cadi came up with a karaoke version of *Digitally Speaking* – a song from the *Journeys End* CD, and as it blasted out of the music hall speakers, I did the vocals. As I walked around the stage, singing my heart out without the use of a mic, I realized that Cadi is right...

I do miss it. A lot...

Having successfully dodged my questions for three days, this morning I trap Cadi in her office, and finally get her to tell me what the real plan is...

The moment she does, I freak.

"*Seal?* You want me to cover *Seal?* Are you nuts? Have you heard the guy's voice? It's past amazing..."

In the middle of my outburst, Martha comes in, stops just inside the door, and laughs.

"No, Emma," Cadi quickly replies, "we don't want a cover. We want you to do the vocals to *our* version of one of his songs."

"Anyone can cover lyrics," Martha adds. "We want something more than that..."

"That's why I asked you." Cadi stands up, comes around her desk, and stops in front of me. "For this to work, we need your *passion,* Emma..."

"Come on," Martha pretty much orders, reaching out and grabbing my arm, "we're set up and we're going to play the song for you – *our way*. At least hear it before you decide..."

"Here," Cadi says, laughing, then handing me some sheet music. The moment I see the title...

"*Seriously?* You want me to sing *this*?"

"Well... yeah..."

As I stand reading the lyrics to *Kiss From A Rose*, my heart races. Truth is, I've always loved the song.

"You guys do realize this song won Record of the Year, *and* Song of the Year, in 1996... right?"

Martha, who is still holding my one of my hands, smiles, and makes me face her.

"I've heard you sing, Emma... and as the good Lord is our witness, you are the one vocalist I know, who can easily do the song justice."

"Now come on," Cadi says, grabbing my other hand and pulling me into the hall, "and listen to it. Then what ever you decide, we'll accept..."

Then next thing I know, I'm standing on the stage, and Walter – the conductor – is bringing them to order. Once they start playing, the lyrics become irrelevant – I *totally* lose myself in the performance.

*It... is... **amazing**!*

Even before the last note fades, I run to the edge of the stage, and yell at Cadi, who along with the rest of the orchestra, is down in the 'pit'.

"I'll do it!"

They all start applauding – including Walter.

"One catch guys," I quickly add, with a big grin covering my face.

"And that would be?" Martha, who is standing next to her seat in the first violin section, asks.

"No orchestra pit. We're all up here..." I point at the stage behind me. *"Together."*

"Done."

I turn to my left and find a gruff-looking, middle aged guy standing next to the curtain controls. As I turn to face him, Cadi walks up next to me.

"Emma, meet Winston. He's our stage manager. Winston, Emma Greene."

"Oh... I know who she is," he replies, his accent even more pronounced than Cadi's. "You want them up here, up here they will be. We'll have the riser and seats in place by tomorrow," he finishes, as he crosses the stage toward us.

"This is going to be amazingly awesome!" I blurt out, suddenly overcome by the excitement of it all – a feeling I haven't had in as long as I can remember.

"No, Miss Greene," Winston offers, as the entire auditorium goes quiet, and all eyes turn to look at the two of us, "as my daughter is so fond of saying, I believe *'it's going to be epic'*."

twenty-two
Stanley

In the middle of teaching a class, I feel my phone vibrate. Because of all the stuff going on, I pull it out, and seeing the Caller ID, quickly answer it, as the kids watch.

"Cadi?"

"Yeah, it's me."

"I'm in the middle of a class here. Can I call you back?"

"Is that the *Audio Distortion* Cadi, Mr. Campbell?" a student in the middle of the room yells out.

"Is it *really* your old bass player?" a second one adds.

"No you can't," Cadi replies, laughing as she does. "Tell them that yes, it's me, I'm definitely NOT old, and I'm your ONLY bass player."

I have to force myself not to laugh.

"*Miss Meredith* says 'yes it's her', that she *isn't old*, and that she's our band's *only* bass player."

I hear a couple of snickers, then the room falls completely silent, and all I can do is stare at them, in total disbelief. My silent hesitation makes Cadi impatient.

"*Stanley!*" I hear from the phone.

"Oh, sorry… that's never happened before."

"What?"

"The whole class quiet at the same time. What's up?"

"I need your butt on a plane and here by Friday – morning. You have to be here Friday morning."

"In England?"

"No you dweeb, Mars. Yes, England."

"Why?"

"Don't ask questions, Stanley. Just say 'okay', and book a flight the moment you hang up."

"Cadi, what the hell is going on?" I blurt out, momentarily forgetting I'm in a room full of high school sophomores.

"I need you here. That's all you need to know. It's important enough, that it could very well affect all our lives. You should probably bring your dad too. I was going to call him next, if you didn't answer."

"Oh my God… you found her."

"Are you coming?"

"On the redeye – probably tomorrow night. My dad and Logan…"

"Just you and your dad for now – *please?* Logan will understand."

"Okay. You going to pick us up?"

"Yes. But there's a condition to all this."

"And that is?"

"No one other than the three of us can know you are here. I intend to bring her home – to Fort Collins – as soon as what we are doing, is finished. Let's do this right, Stanley. Let's make sure she *gets it*. Let's give her a million reasons to accept her destiny…"

"You're the boss. See you in thirty-six hours. And thank you, Cadi – from the depths of my soul.

"See ya."

I flip the phone closed and turn to find eighteen mystified faces staring at me – none of which made a peep during my entire conversation. After a few seconds, a timid little girl in the front row breaks the silence.

"Did Miss Meredith *really* find Miss Greene?"

"That she did, Melody. That she did."

"Wow," comes from a different girl, in the middle of the room, "maybe *Audio Distortion* will *finally* get back together…"

In a matter of seconds, *everyone* is part of a massive conversation about *AD's* 'reunion tour'. The surprising part is, by the end of the day, it has spread to pretty much the entire school.

Kids and social media… what can you do?

As I'm getting ready to leave for the day, Mrs. Marshall wanders into my room, with a huge grin on her face.

"So, Mr. Campbell, should I be looking for a new music teacher?"

"Huh?"

I can tell she is desperately fighting the urge to break up laughing – even if I have no idea why.

"Well, having talked to Midge Polk over at RMHS, and a good friend in Performance Arts at CSU, it seems the current massive rumor that has been consuming most of the educational institutions in the greater Fort Collins area for the last six hours is, *'Audio Distortion is getting back together',* and here on our campus, the main topic of discussion seems to be *'Mr. Campbell going back to being a rock star…'"*

We stand staring at each other, until finally, we break up laughing at the same time.

twenty-three
Stanley

"Stan, I need to tell you something," my dad says, as he pours a little bottle of something over his ice.

"Tell away, Dad. As bizarre as my life has been lately, I'll just add whatever it is, to my growing list of 'weird'."

We're on a plane, going to England, at the insistence of Cadi. I abandoned Willie and Emily in Fort Collins – although both said they understood. Fortunately, Ms. Dreesen was available, and more than happy, to sub for my classes.

"Logan is scared to death," my dad continues, "that something she has done – that she finally told me about two days ago – will scar your relationship with her for good."

"Yeah, right, Dad. I bet it has something to do with Emma, doesn't it?"

"How in the world would you know that?"

"Come on Dad, they are like sisters for crying out loud. They share something the rest of us, don't."

My dad sits there, slowly sipping from his glass, and staring at me.

"So?"

"She knew, Stanley. God knows how, but she knew Emma was going to run – again. She caught her the morning she left..."

I laugh – loudly – for lack of knowing what else to do. The whole situation fits the insanity of our lives, so perfectly.

"Fortunately," my dad continues, "she knew something was up. 'Sisters', 'friends', and all that stuff aside, she made up her mind that she wasn't going to allow Emma to disappear completely – which is what Logan felt she was trying to do."

"Way to go, *Mom*..." I mumble, which makes my dad grin.

"She broke down the other day, and told me what she'd done. She said she woke up that morning with a weird feeling that bothered her so much, she went and sat in Emma's driveway, and waited. When a cab showed up at 7:30 – she knew she was right. She confronted her, and apparently Emma admitted that she intended to sneak off."

He pauses again, and takes another sip from his glass, acting as if he expects some kind of response from me.

"Here's the kicker, Stan..." he says, sucking down the rest of his drink. "For the last two and a half years, not only has Logan known where Emma has been, she's also talked to her twice a month..."

I turn, look my dad in the eyes, and then break into laughter.

"How damn cool is that?"

"That's it?" my dad asks, definitely stunned.

"Yeah, Dad, that's it."

"Okay, Son, I'm going to need an explanation on this one..."

"Because, ever since you gave us that lecture..."

I'm instantly interrupted by my dad laughing.

"...and made me rethink Emma's situation, I've had this very weird vibe. Every so often, when I'm around Logan, it gets more intense. Something – I have no idea what – keeps telling my heart that

Emma is fine... that I don't need to worry. Now... I know why."

I turn, and look out into the total darkness through the open window next to me, using the pause to try and absorb what is happening.

"Just between you and me, I've caught Logan looking at me in a strange way – more than once. It was as if she was waiting for me to ask, or do something... or maybe more like she was *hoping* I would."

I take a deep breath, and turn back to face my father.

"From that moment in the kitchen at Papa Roni's, when Emma took my hand, and I pulled her to her feet, she and I have been 'linked' – as weird as that sounds. That's why, unlike the others, I've never been overly excited about any of this. I've always known – *inside* – that Emma is safe. The weird thing is, my heart also knows that wherever she is, and whoever she's with, *she's happy...*"

He sits staring at me, as if totally unsure how to respond.

"And... for me, Dad, that's enough. It's like you told us, years ago, in the family room – *she has the right to be happy, even if it doesn't include me.*"

"Son, that's by far, the weirdest damn thing you have ever said to me, in the twenty-six years you've been on earth. You are an amazing person, Stanley Campbell."

"Yeah... well... I think that for the first time in my life, I may need a drink. Look..." I hold out my hand so he can see how badly it's shaking.

"Well... okay. I'll buy you a drink. *A drink*," my father replies, smiling, and patting me on the back.

He asks the flight attendant for two bottles of the same thing he has, and a glass of ice. While she is getting it, I pull the phone out of the seat in front of me, and after swiping my credit card, dial.

"That's going to be expensive," my dad says, nodding at what I'm doing.

"Yeah, but your wife doesn't deserve to sit and stew for the next few days either. I need to tell her what she needs to hear – now."

It takes a full thirty seconds before I hear her voice.

"Hey, Logan – it's me."

"Stan... oh... did your dad..."

"Just hush and listen, please?"

"Okay..."

The stress in her voice is so pronounced, I feel really bad for her.

"Let it go, Logan. Okay?"

"Seriously?"

"Yes... seriously. And thank you... from all of us."

After a few seconds of silence, I hear the muffled sobs.

"So," I ask, "are we good?"

"Oh God, Stanley... of course we are. Thank you... for being... well... for..."

"I get it, Logan. Tell Georgia I said 'hey', and I'll talk you to guys when it isn't absurdly expensive, okay?"

"I love you Stan..."

"Back atcha... *Mom...*"

For some strange reason, the moment I hang up, I feel really good. I hold up my hand again, and notice that it isn't shaking any more. I pick up the small bottle and glass of ice the flight attendant left on my table, and when I put them down in front of my dad, he just laughs.

I close my eyes, and lose myself in the thought that, in about twenty-four hours, *I am going to see Emma again* – for the first time, in more than two years.

My heart could pump fluid to the top of a twenty story building at this point...

twenty-four
Emma

The excitement of performing again gets me so wound up, I almost forget about poor Christopher. But, his support never falters.

A couple of times, during rehearsals, I find him in the front row, staring at me, and although I'm not certain, once, he may have actually been crying.

He patiently waits each day – and like tonight, sometimes until after midnight – and walks back to Cadi's with me.

"Emma," he says, as I reach out and take his hand, "I don't get it – I've tried, I swear I have. Having heard you sing, for the life of me I can't understand why you ever quit..."

"Why did you leave Boston?"

It's a game we've been playing since we met – each trying to glean info about the other's past...

Christopher doesn't respond, and we continue up the street in silence...

I know he is quickly fading from me. We haven't been physical at all since we left Italy, and he's even begun to shy away from kissing me, so I've pretty much quit trying.

But, each morning he makes breakfast, and has it waiting on me – and today is no different. When I walk into Cadi's small kitchen, I again try to kiss him, and watch as he carefully avoids the attempt. Now a bit depressed, I take a seat at the table, and watch as Christopher fills my coffee cup. I add some sugar, and slowly stir it, staring at him the entire time.

"After you perform tonight, Emma, I'm going."

"Going where?"

"Back to my life."

"Your real life, or am I being replaced?"

Although made light-heartedly, and in jest, my comment doesn't get the response I expect. Instead, Christopher becomes serious, and takes a seat across from me.

"You're being too nonchalant about this, Emma."

I put my coffee down, then reach out, and take his hand.

"Christopher, come on. You haven't touched me in over a week – including your dodge around the kiss I just tried to give you. You try to appear happy, but we both know you aren't, and on top of all that, you won't talk to me about this. I'm not being nonchalant – just realistic. I want you to be *happy* – no matter what that means."

I pause, and carefully watch his eyes, for any hint of what he might be thinking.

"We've been open and honest with each other for a year and a half, and now isn't the time for that to change. If it is finally time for this to end, and for us to go our own ways, I want it to be on a positive note."

I wait until he finally looks me in the eyes, before I finish my thought.

"Where ever you are, Christopher, if I pop into your head, I want the memory *to make you smile*..."

Still looking quite serious, he stands up, steps around the table, leans over and kisses me. It's the most passionate kiss Christopher has ever given me, and I know it's a 'goodbye' kiss. When it's over, he gently wipes off my lips with his finger, and finally smiles.

"Back to my real life. Back to Boston. Back to face my family. And hopefully, back to finish medical school."

He pauses for a second, and again I find myself wondering what is going on behind his big, brown eyes.

"No more running."

Then, with a devious little smirk on his face, he quickly adds, "And, just for the record, *'replacing'* you, is impossible."

He turns and walks over to the large window in the living room, and stands silently staring out it.

"Do you remember what you asked me, on the way home last night?"

"If you mean the question you didn't answer, then yes."

"I left Boston because I was angry – with my family, with the world, but mostly with myself. I didn't take a stand, and by the time I figured it out, she was gone…"

I can hear the pain in his voice.

"Other people were picking my path, and forcing me to stay on it. In order to ensure I 'fulfilled my destiny' – as my father likes to say – they ran her off, and because *I allowed it*, I lost her…"

I watch him reach up, wipe his cheeks, hesitate for a moment, and then without looking at me, he continues.

"I was so angry, that my response to my father was to disappear – without a word – right in the middle of my second year of medical school."

He finally turns, and again faces me.

"Being with you, has taught me that destiny isn't chosen, it's already set. She's out there – somewhere – and *I have to go find her*. She has always been *my destiny*, Emma, which is why my heart can't seem to let her go..."

He pauses, and after a second, forces a smile.

"How long have you been gone?"

"Two years," I reply.

"And having had enough of your 'silliness', as Cadi put it, *your friends* have come to help you face your destiny."

When I look at him quizzically, he laughs.

"Yeah, we talked... and while she isn't 'admitting' anything, I don't believe for a second, that Cadi is in this on her own..."

Even though I smile at him, my thoughts drift elsewhere.

"And... being the intelligent woman you are, I *seriously* doubt you believe it either."

He makes me laugh... and blush as well.

"In my heart," he continues, "I hope that maybe Courtney and I can do the same – *face our destiny*.

He again pauses, and looks out the window.

"*If...*" he whispers, "I can find her."

I feel the tears coming. Christopher bared his soul, and in doing so, gave me reason to search my own.

"Fair enough. My turn..."

I sit for a moment, and stare at my coffee, actually worried about how he is going to react to what I'm about to tell him.

"Ever since I lost my grandmother, I've had this... well... *'feeling'* I guess, that I'm alone – *totally alone*. There's one thing about me I've never told you..."

I take a deep breath, raise my head, and make eye contact with him.

"*I have no living relatives...*"

His face tells me that it only takes a split second for the reality of what I said to sink in. The instant look of panic and guilt that washes over his face, is exactly what I expect.

"And the look on your face is exactly why I didn't tell you – why I generally don't tell anyone..."

Understanding exactly what I mean, he relaxes, and even lets out a muffled laugh.

"I quit singing because, in my heart, I am deathly afraid that if my destiny even remotely involves losing my voice too, I won't survive. I have no idea if it's true, but hiding from the possibility that destiny can take the only thing I have left, is a lot easier than facing it..."

I feel the tear as it trickles down my cheek.

"So... I stopped singing. I know it's silly, but it seemed reasonable to think that if I don't use it, I can't lose it..."

I stand up, walk to the counter, and refill my cup. I can feel Christopher quietly watching, even though my back is to him.

"Then, one morning, I woke up so totally consumed by a need to be somewhere other than where I was, I simply couldn't fight it. So, just like you, I ran away – and ended up here."

I turn around and again face him, sipping my coffee and hoping for some kind of reaction. When none comes, I keep talking...

"Being with you, on our adventure, gives me a kind of peace of mind... as if I have nothing to lose... nothing that fate and destiny can snatch from me. From the moment it began, we agreed, we'd just..."

He interrupts me, mid-sentence.

"...live in each moment, one day at a time, and when the time comes, will let go and move on."

His response tells me he understands, which allows my heart to finally relax.

"Uh-huh – exactly. We agreed our relationship, while very special, is also finite. In all honesty, I don't want it to end… yet… but if it's time, I'm okay with that."

I feel the tears as they once again begin to trickle down my cheeks.

"We're about a goofy pair – each trying to hide our past, and avoid our destiny… something we know can't be done."

Christopher laughs, and my heart begins to beat normally again.

"We are, and always have been, part of each other's destiny, Christopher. I have thanked God – *every single day since it happened* – for making you turn around on that train…"

I allow myself to smile, put the cup on the counter, cross the room, and when I am within reach, hug Christopher as tightly as I can.

"Promise me you will stay for the concert… please? My heart needs to know you will be out there… listening."

He grabs my arms, gently breaks my grip on his waist, and then pushes me back a couple of steps. Using his finger under my chin, he lifts my head, until our eyes meet.

"Not even death can keep me from being in the front row tonight, lady. You are the most amazing singer I have ever heard. Don't stop, Emma. Don't let this be a one-time thing. Go find Stanley, and the two of you need to rediscover the magic – the magic that allowed you to make music that affected millions of lives for almost a decade."

He leans over and gently kisses my cheek.

"And, you need to rediscover each other as well. I believe you do love me, Emma Greene, but you are – and always have been – ***in love** with Stanley."*

With just a single sentence, he releases my heart, and makes me realize that I was wrong – *that I am ready to let him go, and move on*. He smiles, and gently brushes his hand against my tear-covered cheek.

"*He owns your heart* – just like Courtney has always owned mine…"

He pulls me close, again hugs me, and after only a couple of seconds, he too is crying. Seconds later, over Christopher's shoulder, I see Cadi walk in.

This moment is the closest to panic, I've ever seen her.

twenty-five
Emma

"I need to go find a dress, Cadi. I can't wear jeans and sneakers tonight."

The moment I quit talking, I feel a hand on my shoulder, and see Cadi smile.

"I have a solution for you, Emma," Mrs. Meredith says, from behind me.

I turn to face her, not at all sure what she means.

"Knowing about tonight's' show, my sister called and asked if you might consider allowing her to dress you for your performance?" she says.

"Your sister?"

"My Aunt Seren," Cadi says, smiling.

"My sister is a seamstress, Emma. She creates a number of the traditional Welsh costumes for the eisteddfod in Llangollen each year."

"Like…"

"Yeah, like the one I wore to the studio – way back when," Cadi says, with a laugh.

"Or perhaps…" Mrs. Meredith adds, seeing the look on my face, "something more appropriate for what you are doing?"

"I… uh… well…"

"Oh hush, Emma! Come on…" Cadi reaches out, grabs my hand, and leads me toward the back of her parents' house.

At the end of the hall, we turn into the extra bedroom, and find Cadi's aunt standing next to the bed, with a huge grin on her face, and a beautiful gown lying next to her.

"Hello Emma," she says, as she steps over, and without warning, wraps me up in a hug. "I am quite honored to meet you..."

"Not that big a deal, really..." I reply.

I hear Cadi laugh, and when Seren lets go of me, she steps aside and I get a good look at the dress...

"oh... my... god!" I mumble, as I step over and sit down on the bed next to it. "You *made* this?"

"Of course," she replies, laughing, "it's what I do. You are good with your voice; I am good with a needle and thread."

Still staring at it, I extend my hand toward it, but stop short of touching it. Seeing my hesitation, Mrs. Meredith straightens me out, in a heartbeat.

"Emma, it is simply clothing. Nothing more. You would not be afraid to touch a pair of jeans, would you?"

I hear Cadi laugh behind me, as her aunt steps over and takes one of my hands.

"Yes, Emma, it is made of satin and silk, but it is still *just a dress*. I used Catrin's measurements, as she told me the two of you are close to the same size. If it needs alterations, we can easily do them here – assuming of course you wish to wear it."

"Are you kidding?" I blurt out, as I stand up and carefully pick up the gown. After I glance at Cadi, I turn and walk over to a huge mirror, then stand silently staring at myself, with the dress in front of me. Even as the tears start, I smile and say, "What girl *wouldn't* want to wear this? It's... *amazing*..."

Cadi steps over, and wraps her arms around me from behind, as I again gently run my fingers over the glistening silk of the gown. After giving me a gentle squeeze, she steps back and smiles at me in the mirror.

"Why... white?" I mumble, my fingers still resting on the pink satin ruffles.

"Because," Seren replies, smiling and glancing at Cadi, "of what my sister *and* Catrin have told me of your voice."

"Because, Emma," Mrs. Meredith offers, "when you open your heart and let yourself go, your voice is the *purest* I have ever heard."

As I turn around to face them, Mrs. Meredith takes one of my hands, then reaches out, and puts her other hand on my cheek. "Perhaps, the purity of the white and pink will help you find that voice again... and give it back to a world that has missed it for all these years."

"*You're a singer...*" Cadi whispers, smiling at me.

"And whether I sing or not, I'm always going to be a singer..." I reply, finally understanding.

"Come on, Emma, let's see how it fits! *Off with your clothes...*" Cadi blurts out, breaking the moment.

It takes close to thirty minutes for them to complete their task, and when they put me in front of the mirror again, I'm *completely* overwhelmed.

"*Who knew?*" I mumble, staring at the mountain of white and pink surrounding me.

"Now that we know it fits, and no alterations are required," Seren says, spinning me around and carefully scrutinizing her handiwork, "we will take it to the theater, and will dress you again this evening."

"*Wait...*" I blurt out, turning to face them, and then glancing at Cadi. "Can I just wear it? All day?"

"No, Emma, you can't," Mrs. Meredith says, trying to hide a smirk. "It is not meant to be worn 'out'..."

"But..." Seren adds, turning and opening a closet next to her, "if being beautiful is your intention..."

I hear Cadi crack up laughing, turn to look at her, and find her covering her mouth with both hands. Her mom is also doing her very best not to laugh.

"You could run around in this all day..." I hear from Seren.

When I spin back around, I see she is holding an exact copy of the dress Cadi was wearing when she found me in Italy – except it's the same amazingly brilliant white the gown is.

"No way..." I mumble, as I walk over and look at it. "It looks just like..."

Cadi interrupts me midsentence.

"...this one!"

I turn and find her holding the black and red version of the dress. At this point, the tears simply come, and there's nothing I can do about it. To think that they have gone through all this, for me, touches me in a way I can't explain. Before I know it, Mrs. Meredith is unzipping me, and helping me out of the gown. Once she has it safely on a hanger, I turn in time to see Cadi slipping into her dress. It takes me about a minute to squeeze into the white dress, and again, when I step in front of the mirror, all I can do is shake my head in amazement.

"If you go out in this, Emma, you will draw a lot of attention – just as Catrin does. Are you certain you will be comfortable under such scrutiny?" Mrs. Meredith asks.

"Remember," Seren adds, smiling at me, "there is a great difference between being on stage for a performance, and walking down a busy street."

I again turn and look at myself in the mirror, and smooth out the front of the dress.

"There was a time I would have said 'no' to wearing this out..."

I turn and look at Cadi.

"But now, I actually want to."

"Well then... let's go!" Cadi blurts out, as Seren hands each of us a pair of sandals.

Five minutes later, after a quick brushing of the hair, we head for the living room. The moment Mr. Meredith sees me, he almost freaks.

"Yet another masterpiece, Seren!"

"Byddwch yn anrhydedd i mi..." she replies, although I have no idea what it means.

"Emma, left foot here, please," Mr. Meredith says, tapping on one of the dining room chairs."

I walk over and do as I am told, pulling the dress up enough that my foot is visible.

"This..." he says, holding up a sterling silver anklet with what appear to be two small charms attached to it, "is an exact copy of the one Catrin has worn, since she was ten. As I did with her," he pauses, carefully puts it around my ankle, and closes the clasp, as Cadi and her mom watch, "I give it to you – *father to daughter*."

"Just as Catrin has done, since the day I met her, I too, will try to make you proud," I reply, leaning over and looking at the charms.

"This," Cadi says, leaning over touching the first one, which is as red as her hair, "is *Y Ddraig Goch* – The Red Dragon. It's kinda like the national symbol of Wales."

"And this?" I ask, looking at the second one.

"It's the Triple Harp – or as most of the music world calls it, The Welsh Harp."

"The day I discovered Catrin's love of music, I had the anklet made for her. It allows her to carry two things important to her heritage with her, where ever she may go," her father says.

I put my foot down, and as I turn to face him, Mr. Meredith takes both my hands.

"All that being said, there is something I wish to share with you, if I may. Something deeply personal, and that only those here in this room know."

"Of course," I instantly reply, suddenly overcome by a feeling of apprehensiveness.

"We share a path, Emma. As far back as my memory can take me, I too, was alone. I am... an orphan..."

Totally shocked, I suck in a huge breath, and as I exhale, Mr. Meredith gently squeezes my hands.

"Family, Emma, is in here..." he says, smiling, then reaching out and placing a single finger, over my heart. "When I met Gwendolyn and her family," he points at Cadi's mom, "they knew not of my past, or my origins, but they accepted me... *as family*. My *heart* has never been alone since..."

In a single instant, the ongoing feeling that has been controlling my life – the belief that I am completely alone in the world – simply evaporates. In only thirty seconds, Mr. Meredith does what no one else in my life has been able to, since I lost Grams. With one simple statement, he finally makes me understand and accept that *'family'*, and the bonds that come with it, are *made*, not *inherited*...

I turn and make eye contact with Cadi, and although it's a very weird moment, the look on her face makes it all perfect.

"I feel so foolish, Cadi."

She smiles at me, nods her understanding, then I turn and face the others again.

"Truth is, I was never *really* alone... was I?"

"FINALLY!" Cadi blurts out, her frustration evident.

Mrs. Meredith and her sister step over and hug me at the same time.

"Nor will you even be again, Emma – that is what you must try to remember," Seren says, putting a hand on my cheek. "You have us…"

"And," Mrs. Meredith adds, "you have three other *'families'* that miss your presence in their lives, more than you can know."

Without a word, and grinning from ear to ear, I turn and wrap my arms around Cadi's dad, and he quickly does the same to me.

"This is good. I believe a *daughter* should hug her *father* at least once each day."

"Thank you…" I softly whisper in his ear, "for freeing my soul."

When he lets go of me, I turn back to face Cadi.

"How… how did you know?"

She immediately steps over, wraps both arms around me, and hugs me as tightly as she ever has.

"Because, Emma," she whispers in my ear, "we are, and always have been, *family. All five of us…*"

When she lets go, I smile at her, then turn and again face the others, who are quietly watching.

"And… thank you – *all of you.* Today has been the most amazing experience of my life so far. I can only hope that tonight, with my voice, I'll make you…" I turn and look directly at Cadi's dad, "proud of me."

"Of that, Emma," Mr. Meredith says, following it with a laugh, "there is no doubt. I *have* heard you sing before…"

"And…" Seren quickly adds, a big smile covering her face, "as Catrin so eloquently put it earlier, I am prepared to be 'blown away' this evening."

Her comment makes everyone – me included – laugh…

"Come on," Cadi says, kissing her dad's cheek, and then taking my hand, "I know the perfect place for lunch... and there are always lots of guys hanging around. Let's go practice our flirting... shall we?"

Seren laughs, Mr. Meredith rolls his eyes, and Mrs. Meredith shakes her head.

In the entire twenty-six years of my life to date, I never got as much attention – including two young boys who give us a 'WOW' as we cross a street – as I do walking the single mile to the cafe. And, although thoughts of Christopher do pass through my mind, my heart tells me that he will totally understand.

Oh... and just so you know – having to be *careful* when eating, generally takes all the fun out of the process.

twenty-six
Stanley

Cadi's dad met us at the airport, and took us to a hotel, six blocks from the concert hall. Just before we went in to register, Mr. Meredith also gave me a note from Cadi.

I'm so burnt out from flying that, once in the room, I actually sleep soundly, for close to ten hours.

Because we can't be 'seen', Dad and I hide out in our room, with the exception of a couple of trips to the restaurant next to the hotel. We're having a late lunch when, still a bit apprehensive, I finally make myself read the note...

Stanley,

*The first thing you need to know, is that yes, there's a guy. I'm going to leave it at that for now. I just didn't want it to be a shock if... well, you get the idea. I'm hoping that for one night, you'll see past all that. This had to be done a certain way, and I can only hope you will trust me. My father will get you to your seats, which are fairly close to the stage, center section. **No one** can know the two of you are here. Yes, there is a reason, and being the overly intelligent guy you are, I'm willing to bet you'll figure it out at* some point. If you don't, I promise to explain, once I get her back to Fort Collins. By now, you know that Logan helped me find her. Although she hasn't said anything yet, I'm pretty sure Emma realizes it too. Emma is the most understanding and kind-hearted person I've ever known, and I'm certain she won't let this mess up her relationship with Logan.

Even through all the secrecy, my heart knows that you, and your dad, need to be here. My heart also knows that the two of you will understand, and will give me some space on this.

A week, Stanley, that's all I'm asking for. We are, and always will be, family...

Catrin

p.s. I've watched her rehearse this. I suggest you hold on to your heart, Stanley Campbell!

I smile, hand the note to my father, and go back to eating.

As weird as it all has been to this point, I am for some reason, totally calm and relaxed. I just need to see her – even if only for a few minutes. Once that happens, I'll do exactly as Cadi asks – go home and wait.

"You okay with this, Stan?" my dad asks.

"Uh-huh... I am. "

"And what about this 'guy' she mentioned?"

I laugh, I can't help it.

"Dad, there have been three girls in *my* life over the last few years – heck you bought the last one dinner on her birthday. How is that any different?"

I stop and wash down the food in my mouth with a drink.

"I just need to know she's happy – no matter what that means."

Again, I baffle my dad. He shakes his head, and takes the last bite of food from his plate.

"I am curious about what song she could possibly be singing, that would be accompanied by a full orchestra…"

"Yeah," my dad says, wiping his face and tossing the napkin on his empty plate, "I've been wondering the same thing since you first told me she was performing with an orchestra."

"Well… we'll get an answer in about…" I twist my wrist and look at my watch, "six hours. The suspense is killing me."

"Oh sure it is, Stanley… sure it is."

We both start laughing.

twenty-seven
Emma

It takes Seren and Mrs. Meredith a full thirty minutes to get me dressed again – plus another fifteen to get my hair the way they want it. I even catch an interesting twinkle in Cadi's eyes, as the two of them fuss over me. I'm just fascinated with the fact they're putting so much effort into *me*...

Now... it's *show time*.

The orchestra has finished their scheduled repertoire, and once they get rearranged Walter will introduce me.

I pull off the sandals, lay them on a chair, and walk over to the orchestra riser. When Cadi sees me coming she stands up, and meets me.

"Remember what you asked me... at that table in Torino?"

She laughs, reaches out, and takes my hands.

"Yes..."

"The answer is yes, I miss it more than I will ever be able to explain to anyone. *You*, Catrin Meredith, made me see that."

"We – the five of us – are a band Emma. *It's what we do.* And, just like *family*, it's a bond that doesn't just go away. We are, and *always will be* – no matter what paths we travel, or what complications life throws at us – *Audio Distortion*..."

Once again, I hug her, and when we break the embrace, Cadi laughs, and points at my 'back-up' singers, who are standing near their mics.

We snatched the four of them – spur of the moment – from a local choir. They were more than willing and quite excited at the chance to perform – especially when I told them what song we were going to sing.

Although I know they'll be awesome, one of them is having a case of nerves like I had – years ago, in the back room of a pizzeria.

"You should probably go talk to Mona…"

I turn and walk over to them, feeling more excited than I have in as long as I can remember. When I hear the older girls trying to reason with Mona, it makes me laugh, and they all turn and look at me.

"*Girls*… seriously. We are going to be *awesome!* Relax, and go with it. You know the song, we've practiced the harmonies. Tonight is just another rehearsal, okay?"

I take a breath, then reach out and take Mona's hand, and gently squeeze it.

"Mona, you're an amazing vocalist – that's why I asked for your help. Let everything else go, and put yourself in church. None of this…" I wave my arm to indicate everything around us, "…matters. *He*…" I pause and point straight up, "…doesn't need to be impressed. He just wants each of us to *use* the gifts He's given us. So tonight, the five us, are going to…"

The other girls all jump right in…

"*SING!*" five voices say at the same time, making some of the orchestra members laugh.

The girls on either side of Mona each put an arm around her shoulders.

"*We are going to be brilliant, Mona!*" one of them says, making the others giggle.

Then we hear Walter…

"Ladies and gentleman, sons and daughters, tonight the Churchtown Community Orchestra and Concert Center is proud and honored to present, in a one-time appearance, Miss Emma Greene."

The lights go out, throwing the entire auditorium into both silence and darkness, and the curtain rises. The moment the curtain begins to move, I turn on my mic, take hold of both Mona's hands, and wink at her.

When the curtain stops moving, a single spotlight illuminates the five of us from directly above, and we immediately begin the song's opening harmony.

And, as strange as it is, Mona *completely* relaxes, the moment we start singing. I suppose music can do that to you, especially if you're passionate about it.

Seconds later, the orchestra joins us, and once they light the entire stage, I turn to the audience and deliver *Kiss From A Rose* with more passion and power, than any song I have ever performed.

The audience gets every ounce of Emma Greene, I have to give.

The moment I sing the last line, and the lights again go out, it occurs to me that Winston – the stage manager – had been right about one thing...

It...
Is...
Epic!

twenty-eight
Stanley

The moment the light hits her, my heart stops. Although I've seen Cadi – and even Vicki – 'dressed-to-kill' on more than one occasion, the gown Emma is wearing, eclipses it all. In the twenty-six years I've been on earth, I've never seen *anything* as beautiful as Emma is, at this moment...

Then... I hear her voice. Although the opening harmony contains five voices – which I should point out, are amazingly perfect together – my mind quickly separates Emma's. When she starts her solo, I close my eyes, and completely lose myself...

Halfway through the performance, I turn and look at my dad – and for maybe the second or third time in my life, am actually shocked.

He's sitting straight up, hands clasped, fingers interlocked, staring directly at the stage. If it weren't for the tears trickling down his cheeks, I might have thought the guy was dead. The only other time in my life I've see him cry openly, was the day he married Logan – at the exact moment she said 'I do'.

When she reaches the last verse, with the help of two of her backup singers, Emma carefully goes to her knees in front of their mic stands, and again all the lights go out. Two heartbeats later, a single, narrow spot lights just her, and she sings the last four lines 'a cappella'. As she lowers her head, *all* the light goes out, throwing the entire auditorium into almost complete darkness.

Once the final note fades completely, there is an eerie, hanging silence, for a good ten seconds, and it seems as if everyone in the building is holding their breath.

Then, the audience – which is less than 400 people – responds, and it surpasses anything I have ever seen, *in my entire life* – including arenas with 15,000 people in them.

When the lights come up again, *everyone* is immediately on their feet applauding, whistling and yelling. At the same time, a line of people with flowers, begins to form, and in only seconds, extends halfway up the main aisle, and keeps growing.

We watch as the entire orchestra, comes to their feet, and begin to applaud as well. Then, the conductor lays his baton on the podium, steps down, walks directly over to Emma, bows, and then helps her to her feet. She pulls off her wireless mic, hangs it from one of the mic stands, then turns and hugs each of the girls behind her.

Poor Emma is lost – I've seen the same look on her face many a time. The response is far past anything she's expecting.

Out of nowhere, my father turns and hugs me – tighter than he ever has before. When I look into his eyes, I realize what has happened.

Emma Greene has unknowingly just given my father, the greatest gift she could have. For the first time in his life, a piece of music has reached in – *all the way in* – and touched my dad.

I turn back to the stage in time to see the conductor, leading Emma – with the other four girls right behind her – up to the front edge, where the five of them, arms around each other and tears running down their cheeks, take repeated bows together. After a few moments, with the help of one of the girls, Emma once again goes to her knees, at the edge of the stage.

One after another, people give her flowers – everything from large bouquets, to single roses – in what seems like an endless procession. Emma, completely overwhelmed, thanks each person, and hands the flowers to the girls behind her. And, of course, she's sobbing the entire time.

Standing here, a huge smile covering my face, I realize that for some strange reason, I don't feel a need to rush down to the stage. I thought I'd have to force myself to adhere to Cadi's rule of Emma not knowing we are here, but that isn't the case. I am truly content to stand next to my dad, and watch, as the world recovers one of its missing vocalists...

And, I am immensely thankful that Cadi made sure we got the chance to see it.

Then, by sheer chance, I notice something. Something I've seen a thousand times before, in a thousand different places.

The press. Not the local press... the real press.

I quickly scan the crowd near the stage and am totally stunned as, within a matter of seconds, I pick out at least five faces I recognize.

"*What the hell?* How do *they* know about this...?"

Hearing my comment, my dad quickly turns and looks at me. Still checking for familiar faces, in a single moment of perfect clarity, my proverbial 'light bulb' goes on – and, just as Cadi said, I 'figure it out'.

I look in the direction of the orchestra's riser, and there, sitting alone, wiping the tears off her face and watching Emma, is Miss Catrin Meredith.

"Lady... you just shot right to the top of my 'Most Devious Females' list."

I start laughing again, and my dad speaks up.

"Stanley?"

I take a single step over next to him, so he can hear me over the crowd noise.

"Cadi is far more devious than I could have ever imagined, Dad. Want to know why no one can know we're here?"

"Sure..."

"I'm guessing it's because Catrin Meredith wants this to spin in a very specific way when it's over..."

"Huh?"

I raise my arm and point into the crowd near the stage.

"See the brunette with all the curls?"

"Yeah..."

"Amanda Simmons – *LA Times music reporter*. Opposite side of the stage..." I point a different direction, "...the guy with the note book?"

"Uh huh..."

"James Wolf of Q Magazine. And the guy with the pony tail he's talking to? Pete McCollum of MOJO."

"Stan... how the..." my father starts to say, now understanding what I'm implying. I interrupt him mid-sentence.

"It gets even better, Dad..." I continue, once again adjusting the direction I'm pointing, "...the killer blonde over there, in the shadows, near the stage curtain, *with the cameraman*..."

"Jezzz, Stanley..."

"Teddi Watkins – *Rolling Stone Magazine*..."

Now on the verge of freaking out, my dad turns and looks me right in the eyes – which, of course, makes me crack up. In the middle of laughing I again raise my arm, point in a new direction, and when my dad turns his head to follow my finger, his eyes find Cadi – still sitting alone, and still crying.

"That, Dad, is the most devious woman I have ever had the pleasure of knowing. And, we need to get out of here before one of them recognizes me. Whatever she's up to, I don't want to screw it up. Come on."

Ninety seconds later, we're walking along in silence, headed for the hotel. Neither of us says a word for the entire six block walk. In truth, there isn't anything to be said.

Emma's performance said it all.

We are on our way home at 10:00 AM the next morning and, for the first time I can remember, I actually fall asleep on a plane.

I spend the next five hours having the most awesome dreams about the woman that – one way or another – *I fully intend to marry…*

twenty-nine
Emma

After it's over, Walter and Martha – followed closely by Cadi – take me backstage to an empty office, and make me lie down on a small couch.

Yes, it all gets to me... *big time*.

"Slow your breathing, Emma," Martha says, as she slips a small pillow under my head, "or you are going to hyperventilate."

"The doctor will be here momentarily," Walter offers, his concern visibly evident.

Cadi steps past them, and sits down on the edge of the couch, next to me. With a smile, she reaches out and wipes the tears off my cheeks.

"*Well...* there certainly isn't going to be any living with you, after *that* performance..."

Martha giggles and Walter tries not to laugh.

"Cadi... it's just a song... it isn't even my song... I don't understand..." I mumble, trying to do as Martha said, and slow down, my now quite erratic breathing.

In the middle of my comment, there's a knock at the door, and everyone turns to look. First, a middle age guy I assume is the doctor comes in. Seconds later, Winston appears at the still-open door. Martha is the first to notice his tears.

"Winston – what's wrong? Are you okay?"

"One sec there, Doc..." Winston says, moving past Martha without responding to her. He comes directly across the room, kneels next to the couch, and carefully takes one of my hands. After glancing at Cadi, he gives my hand a gentle squeeze, takes a really deep breath, lets it out slowly, and looks me right in the eyes.

Here's the strange thing... the moment Winston takes my hand, I instantly slow down, and my world refocuses. Even my erratic breathing subsides.

"Miss Greene..."

I giggle the moment he says it, I can't help myself.

"Winston... seriously... at this point you should be using my first name – don't you think?"

My comment makes Cadi and Martha laugh, and Winston blush.

"*Emma* – everyone here will tell you, I'm a gruff, crass, ornery old guy who generally never shows a bit of emotion. *Performers* usually do nothing more than get on my nerves...

"But, the moment you insisted the musicians *share the stage* with you, I knew you were different. I knew that with you, it was about the *performance* – not the *performer*.

"You – *your performance* – touched something in me. It was brilliant!"

He reaches up and wipes a few tears from his cheeks.

"Tonight, Emma, was what music *should always be about*..."

I push myself up slightly, keeping my feet on the couch, and holding tightly to Winston's hand.

"Music, should always be about *the passion*..."

He smiles, lifts my hand, gently kisses it, then stands up, and goes toward the door, without another word. I call out to him as he reaches the door.

"Winston..."

He pauses and turns back to face me.

"Was your daughter here tonight?"

"She was! She and her best friend were in the second row, center."

"Was she right?" I ask, grinning.

"Most assuredly, Miss Greene," he replies, with a laugh. "It was indeed, *epic!*"

He turns, and goes out the door, leaving the rest of them laughing. The doctor steps over and holds out his hand to me.

"Miss Greene, I want you to take these…" he says, putting three pills in my hand, "…and lie here quietly for at least an hour. The rest of you…" he turns and looks around the room, "…need to go away and let her rest and slow down."

"Doctor, I appreciate…"

That's as far as I get, before he glares at me, immediately cutting of any further resistance I might consider offering. I quickly toss the pills into my mouth, take the glass of water he offers, and wash them down.

"He does that to us too, Emma," Cadi says, as she takes the glass from me and stands up. "See you in an hour."

They're all laughing as they leave the room, the doctor turning off the lights just before he closes the door.

thirty
Emma

An hour turns into two and a half. It is just after midnight when I hear Cadi's voice...

"Emma..."

Then... I'm being shaken.

"Emma... time to wake up girl..."

As I slip back into consciousness, I slowly open my eyes.

"Hey... how you doing?"

Cadi takes my hand, and helps me sit up.

"I was asleep... musta been a dream..."

Cadi laughs, as I swing my legs over the edge of the couch.

"You couldn't be that lucky. I brought your clothes from the house."

I pull my hair out of my face, and look to see that my jeans, a shirt, and my Nikes are stacked in the chair next to me.

"Why, Cadi?" I ask, standing up, and letting her help me get out of the gown. "I honestly don't get it... I just sang a song..."

"Do you remember the day this all started? The very first time the five of us played together?"

"Of course..."

"When you saw all those people standing around listening, you just kept singing, remember?"

"Uh-huh. I also remember being petrified."

"And what did Maggie say when she came out of the crowd just before you bolted for the kitchen?"

"'OMG – Wait till I tell my dad we have a freakin' house band!'"

Cadi laughs, and shakes her head.

"And then?"

Her question makes me blush, because I know where she's going...

"She commented on my voice..."

"Yes, *your voice*. She said, *'Emma, you have an amazing voice, and your band totally rocks!'* Thing is, the band came *after* your voice."

I lean over, tie my sneakers, and then put my hair back into a ponytail, as Cadi carefully puts the gown on a hanger, and then on a hook, on the back of the door.

"The very first time Ms. Dreesen came to watch us practice, what was the first thing she said... the first thing *she* commented on?" Cadi asks, crossing the room and stopping in front of me.

"Okay... okay... you made your point!" I blurt out.

"Even without us – without the band – you should still be sharing your voice, Emma. You just proved you can sing *anything*..."

"No way, Cadi. It's not going to happen. Tonight was about my friend asking me for a favor..."

"So... *'the past is behind you'* and all that silly garbage?"

I realize what she's doing, and knowing I have no defense for it, I sit staring at her.

"Remember that table in Torino? Remember my response to leaving the past behind?"

I continue to stare, completely at a loss, knowing I'm inevitably going to lose this one...

"It's what you and Chris are doing – trying to lose yourselves in your adventure, so you can forget the past – yours *and* his."

She pauses, her eyes locked to mine, as if in a standoff of wills – which of course, she knows she is winning.

"Remember twelve hours ago, in my parents' living room?"

I nod in response.

"You've sorted that out. So why keep running? Look me in the eyes Emma, and tell me you want to go back to the life you've been living, and I'll let this go… right now."

I reach up and wipe a couple of small tears off my cheeks, and continue to stare at her.

"It's time – *for both of you* – to stop running."

Again, she pauses.

"If Chris is your future, we – *Stanley included* – will accept him without question, because that's what family does. I would think you'd know that."

She pauses again, and I see tears on *her* cheeks.

"We – Willie, Emily, Stan, and I – just want our friend back, Emma… Please…?"

For the second time in as many days, Catrin Meredith has seen through all my camouflage and defenses – and at that exact moment, I hate her…

Well… okay, not hate – exactly.

"That's twice, Cadi," I say, forcing a smile. "You really need to quit seeing through me – it's getting seriously annoying."

"The only reason I can call you on any of that, is because I'm guilty of the exact same thing – hiding. For me, it's been living a non-descript life, with a small orchestra, in rural England. Martha made me see that…"

She steps over and sits down next to me on the couch, and puts a hand on my knee.

"We – *the five of us* – have foolishly let the connection we shared, slip away from us. We need to find our way back to being the friends we were, for seven years."

She smiles, then reaches out, and takes my hand.

"And you… you need to sing, damn it. Even if it's without us."

"Have you ever given any thought to where we'd be, if the four of you hadn't come into that kitchen and talked me out of that silly storage room, Cadi?"

She just smiles at me.

"I have – every single day, for the last three years. Without the four of you to bail me out, each time I've collapsed, I wouldn't be here – I honestly believe that.

"This – all of it – started because of the four of you. Without your faith in me, I would have been 'just another girl in college'. Every stage I've ever been on has been with you guys, and because of you guys. If the four of you aren't part of it, there's really no reason for me to do it."

Although I'm looking at her, my mind is back inside Papa Roni's… all those years ago.

"If I sing for audiences again, it will be with the four of you. Period."

The huge smile that spreads across her face makes me instantly suspicious – and of course makes me smile too.

"So…" she says, a definite gleam in her eyes, "if you *were* to get onstage again, the four of us will have to be with you?"

"Or, like tonight," I reply, "one of you would have to goad me into it."

She sits silently staring at me, as if lost for a moment, in a world of her own.

"And what about you, *Catrin Meredith*..." I almost whisper, "*Are you ready to be onstage again?*"

The moment her eyes glass over, my heart races.

Could, what I suspect, actually be happening?

"It's taken me three years, and an innocent comment my best friend made, to make me realize that I've been ready since the day after we 'went our own ways'. Although God gave me the gift of music, I believe He always intended I use it to make *our* kind of music... the orchestra was only a path to get me there."

"Seriously, Cadi? You think we made a mistake letting it go?"

"No, Emma, stopping wasn't the mistake. We *needed* a break from it, and from each other. The mistake was not going back to doing what we are exceptionally good at..."

"Making music... *and*... being friends..."

"Exactly."

"And now... they have jobs, different lives, and even, *kids*. I think we've missed our chance, Cadi..."

The grin that spreads across her face, and the small tears now trickling from the corners of her eyes, quickly confirm my suspicions, and I realize that Christopher was absolutely right. They're *all* – not just Cadi – in this up to their eyeballs.

"Do we really have any right to mess with that?" I ask, trying desperately to keep a straight face.

"I can't believe the single greatest supporter of the 'destiny theory' I've ever met, just asked that question."

Even as a feeling of euphoria sweeps over me, it takes every ounce of willpower I can muster, not to fall into hysterical laughter. *Family*... it seems, is a very magical thing – and this proves that mine, is *amazing*.

"I need to ask something, Emma," Cadi says, changing the subject suddenly. "You don't have to answer, but I'm hoping you will."

"Okay?"

"Where did tonight come from? I've seen you pour yourself into lots of performances – *A Hard Road* the night we lost Grams, the night at Moby Arena, when Matt put you on the spot, and the night we finally sang *We Are* for an audience. But tonight was past all of it. Where did it come from?"

I laugh – mostly because I know she's baiting me.

"You know good and well where it came from, Catrin Meredith. You picked that particular song because you knew where I'd go – inside – to get it."

The moment the little smirk shows itself, I know I'm right – about all of it.

"Yes, Cadi, it was Stanley. All the way to the last word, it was about Stanley."

She smiles, leans over and hugs me, obviously fighting back tears. When she lets go of me, I stand up and pull her to her feet as well.

"Well, I've already booked our flight home…"

"Home?"

"Yeah… *home*," Cadi quickly replies, giving me an obnoxious look. "To Fort Collins. We leave Tuesday."

"Don't *you* live here?" I ask, for no reason other than to provoke her.

"For the time being…" she instantly shoots back, a devious little smirk now covering her face.

"I see," I reply, fighting the urge to laugh. "And we're going to Fort Collins because…"

"I promised to help Willie with something, but had to postpone it to go find you. You know me and promises…"

"I do."

"And… I booked three seats, so you can bring Chris."

The moment she says it, I laugh again. Although her confusion is evident, I offer no explanation, but instead change the subject. I know she's going to find out soon enough…

"I'm starving, Cadi – think we can find some food on the way back to your place?"

"I know the perfect place – it's open late, and we can sneak in the back…" Cadi replies, turning toward the door.

"So, that's what I've been resigned to – sneaking in the back?"

Cadi opens the door, waits for me to step through, and follows me into the hall. She locks the door, and then heads down the hall toward the exit at the end, with me close behind. As we step through the exit, into the cool air of an English fall night, she answers my last question.

"'Sneaking' will become common place when you find out what else I've done, Emma…"

We head down the street, arm in arm, laughing.

And yes, although Cadi never mentions it, I'm sure she notices that Christopher is missing…

thirty-one
Stanley

Logan is waiting for us at the airport, and the first thing I do, is hug her.

"Thanks."

"Thanks?"

"Yeah, thanks. Thanks for being smarter than the rest of us, and giving Emma what she needed – in a controlled fashion."

I hear my dad laugh, which makes me laugh.

"You aren't angry with me?"

"Come on, Logan... *she's Emma*..."

She and Dad laugh.

"And... even if you told us where she was... what would that have changed? You managed to give her what she needed, and give us what we needed when the time came. We both know that if you'd done it any differently, we might have actually lost her. Even though it took two years, *we had to let her find herself...*"

She smiles, her eyes again cloud up, and then she hugs me.

"So?" she asks, once she lets me go.

"Based on what we saw, there's no doubt she found *something*. It was so off-the-chart, she actually made Dad cry."

Logan immediately turns and looks at my dad.

"There isn't an adjective to adequately describe what that young woman did. I've watched her perform a thousand times, Logan – but this eclipsed it all. Even as it was happening, all I could think of was 'how could Logan miss this?'"

"He's right. For three years you've been her anchor. More than any of us, *you* should have been there..."

"Well... someone made sure I was. Actually, someone made sure most of the music world was," she says, pulling out her phone, pushing some buttons, and then handing it to me.

A video of Emma's performance is playing on the small screen, and the moment I see the angle of the image, I know it was shot by Teddi Watkins' cameraman. After a second, I realize it's a news report...

> *After more than three years out of the music spotlight, Emma Greene – lead singer of the pop-music phenomenon, Audio Distortion – has apparently reemerged. Based on a rumor, a number of music reporters slipped into the sleepy little suburb of Churchtown – just outside Southport, England, only to discover that Miss Greene was in fact there. What was rumored to be an impromptu performance to benefit a local private school, turned out to be anything but...*

The camera cuts back to a close up of Emma, in the middle of one of the choruses, fists clenched, singing her heart out, as the announcer continues...

> *Tonight, Miss Greene showed the members of this small community – as well as the rest of the world – that accompanied by a pop band, or in this case, a full orchestra, her voice stills works just as beautifully as it ever did.*

"Catrin Meredith, you are an insanely devious woman..." I mumble, fighting back a laugh. I turn, and look over my shoulder at my dad, who has a big smirk on his face.

"Remember my comment about 'spin'?"

He laughs.

"Cadi did this?" Logan asks, taking her phone back, when I hold it out.

"Uh-huh... she certainly did – all by herself. And... I'll *never again* question any plan the girl comes up with."

"So what now?" my dad asks, as we turn and head for Logan's truck.

"Cadi said to give her a week – so, we give her a week."

"If she pulled this off, I find myself wondering if we should be worried..." my dad says, putting an arm around my shoulders.

"Dad, I think the word you are looking for here... is 'scared'. Should we be *scared...*"

All of us break up laughing...

thirty-two
Emma

We make it back to Cadi's apartment just after 2:00 AM. Now having a full stomach, I'm ready to get some sleep, knowing that the next few days are going to be insane. As we approach the door, we see something hanging in the center of it.

"Your fans have found you, Emma," Cadi says, laughing and pulling off what turns out to be a big red heart, folded in half.

Even as she unfolds it, I know it has nothing to do with 'fans', and when her facial expression changes in an instant, I put both arms around her from behind, and hug her.

"It's okay, Cadi. I knew…"

She looks at me, her worry and concern evident.

"May I?" I ask, gently pulling it out of her hands.

I unfold it, pull loose the key taped inside it, and open the door. Cadi follows me in, and closes the door behind her.

"You knew?"

"Yes. Like you said earlier, now is as good a time as any – *for both of us* – to quit running. Besides, he has someone he has to find."

When I glance at her, the look of total confusion on her face almost makes me laugh.

"We knew it was going to end, Cadi – from the day it started. That's what made it work. It was exactly what both of us needed – for a while. Now, he needs to find the love of his life – and I need to get back to mine… *I hope.*

I smile and wink at her, which I think adds to her confusion. She takes off her coat, as I walk over and drop onto the couch, still holding the heart.

"Although I did make him promise to stay for the concert," I say over my shoulder, "when I looked for him while everyone was giving me flowers, his seat was empty. I'm pretty sure he had a plane to catch…"

After I think about it for a few seconds, I open the giant heart, and read what Christopher has written…

> It was the most amazing performance I have ever seen. Period.
> For God's sake, Emma, don't cheat the world. Please.
> Take Cadi, go find Stanley and the rest of them, and MAKE MUSIC ~ all of you!
> It's your destiny girl. It's their destiny.
> It always has been. You taught me that.
> For the rest of time, if I hear kiss from a rose, my mind will always drift back to a small concert hall, in England.
> You will live forever, in my heart, and in my memories. There's no doubt, that when you 'pop into my head', I will be smiling.
> And… if you are ever in Boston…
>   Christopher

Strangely enough, I don't cry. Instead, as I hand the note to Cadi, who is trying to read it over my shoulder, I close my eyes and silently ask God to make *certain* Christopher finds Courtney.

"I'm so confused," she says, handing it back to me.

"Welcome to *my* world, Cadi…"

Even though I said it, truth is, for the first time in close to five years, I'm not confused… or scared… or even nervous.

With the help of Christopher, Mr. Meredith, and Cadi, everything has become crystal clear.

I *finally* understand exactly where my future lies…

thirty-three
Stanley

"You guys ready to do this?"

"Nope."

I look directly at Melinda.

"What do you mean, *'nope'?*"

"Someone got sick, so Randi had to go be in her sister's wedding – which is cool, but now we don't have a bass player," Melinda replies.

They've been practicing like crazy, and we – Willie, Emily and I – want to see them play. *We* know they're ready.

"Damn…"

"It's cool, Mr. Campbell," Patty says, smiling at me. "Chuck…" she points at a kid standing next to Pete's keyboard, "and his band said they'll cover for us. We'll get another chance after school starts again…"

"HEY!" we hear at the same time, from a British sounding female voice, in the shadows. "I hear you guys need a bass player…"

The kids spin around, and find themselves face to face with the still extremely hard to understand, Miss Catrin Meredith – the highly skilled bass player of the pop group *Audio Distortion* – clad in jeans, a new pair of sneakers, a tank-top, and sporting the *coolest* pair of bright red pigtails.

And of course, the pigtails should have been the first clue – the last time I saw her, she had too much hair for pigtails…

Now, one would think that, based on the rest of the clues – our phone call, and the note Cadi sent that day in Southport – I would grasp the meaning of her presence *on stage at a high school, in Colorado...*

But, in my usual haphazard, space-cadet manner, it goes right over my head...

"NO WAY!" Pete blurts out.

"SERIOUSLY DUDE!" comes from Melinda, just as quickly.

"Jezzz... what the heck is it with the three of you? Every time I turn around, one of you is sneaking into my life!" I blurt out, making everyone within earshot crack up – including the kids.

"The fact it appears to be so easy to sneak up on you, should tell you something, Stanley," Cadi replies, grinning at me.

She turns to the totally stunned kids, and says, "So... do you guys need a bass player, or should I run along?"

"o... m... g..." Melinda mutters, really slowly.

"Are you serious? *You're* gonna play the dance with us?" Patty asks.

Pete, standing at his keyboard, his mouth open, actually appears to be paralyzed, and it takes all of my willpower, not to fall into hysterical laughter.

"If you want me to, I'd be honored. Willie and Emily say you guys kick butt. I'd like to see that for myself..."

When no one says anything, Cadi steps over to Pete's keyboard and asks, "Set list?"

With a shaky hand, he holds out a single sheet of paper to her.

"I know this one... and this one... and I certainly should know this one – I've played it a thousand times."

"It's the last one, Cadi... that's the one they are worried about. Pete's dad is here to hear them play it. They've only rehearsed it with Randi on bass..."

"Sheet music?"

Without a word, Pete hands her more pages. I know she doesn't need the music – the girl can ad-lib any bass line on earth, with little or no effort. She's just playing the game with them. Watching it makes me remember why I love teaching, as much as I love making music.

As Cadi reads, a figure comes out of the shadows behind her, and stops next to her.

"Uh... excuse me," comes from little Miss Sally Wright, standing in the shadows, looking near panic.

"Yes?" I reply.

She smiles at me, but turns to face the kids in the band.

"I was wondering... if you guys *are* going to play after all, would you consider letting me sing for you? Maybe? I mean... if you still think I can do it..."

Before anyone can answer her, Cadi spins around, and hands her the set list.

"Do you know all those songs?"

"Oh, yes ma'am," Sally replies, grinning and already beginning to blush, "I know all of them. I'm always hanging around when they practice. And..." she pulls a folded sheet of paper out of her back pocket, "I've even memorized the new song."

"no way..." Pete mumbles as a grin spread across his face.

As Sally is fighting the battle with her nerves, without warning, Patty and Melinda leap into the air and scream simultaneously.

"OH HECK YEAAAAHHH!"

It's abrupt and so loud, it makes me jump.

"What?" I yell, turning to look at them.

Patty, drumsticks in hand, a huge grin on her face, walks over and stops right in front of me.

"Are you kidding, Mr. Campbell? With Sally doing the vocals, and Miss Meredith playing bass, we are *soooo* totally going to destroy this place tonight!"

She turns to Chuck, who himself looks pretty much zoned.

"I know we were gonna trade…"

"Are you *freakin' nuts*, Patty?" he instantly replies. "This is gonna be like so totally *epic!* I'm gonna go find a spot right up front!"

Everyone laughs as Chuck reaches out, bumps fists with Patty, and then turns and disappears off stage. I, in turn, step over and kneel down in front of Sally – who is all of five feet tall. Maybe.

"You certain you're up to this?"

Sally, with the cutest grin on her face, looks me right in the eyes.

"I honestly don't know, Mr. Campbell, but these guys…" she turns and points at the other kids, "…seem to think I can do it, so we might as well find out."

At a complete loss, I smile, and hand the kid a microphone. As I stand up, Melinda and Patty walk over, and stop next to Sally.

"You remember what we told you during the last practice?" Patty asks.

"About the crowd?" Melinda adds.

"Close my eyes and ignore them?" Sally replies, grinning.

"It always works for me, Sally!" Cadi offers, putting a hand on her shoulder.

Shaking my head, I go to introduce them.

"Okay guys and girls – you ready for some live music?"

The second they hear me, the kids rush toward the portable stage we put in the gym once a month, for dances. I wait for the cheering to slow down, and then introduce the kids.

"Tonight, for your dancing pleasure, Fort Collins High presents… *'Saturday Afternoon!'*"

Their band name cracks me up – although it's fitting. They met for the first time, on a Saturday afternoon, at one of my freshman orientations.

They start playing their first song, even before the curtain opens, and when the crowd sees Cadi and Sally, they go nuts. For the next thirty minutes, there isn't a single stationary body in the entire building.

Including mine.

I find myself dancing with a couple of the chaperoning mothers… which cracks the kids up.

They're getting ready to play their last song – the one they wore themselves out perfecting – when Pete's dad walks up to me.

"Thanks, Mr. Campbell – Pete and Patty told us how much effort you put into helping them learn this song."

"Not me," I reply, smiling and pointing at Willie and Emily, "them."

"None the less, without you, my son would not have the passion he does for music. You make a bigger difference than you will ever understand."

Just as he finishes talking, his son walks up to the mic, and we turn our attention to him.

"Dad, at first this was for you and in a way, it still is. But it has become about a lot more than that. Thanks for supporting my music."

Then it's Melinda's turn.

"Miss Táo and Mr. Morgan – wherever you are – will you guys please come up here?"

The two of them immediately look right at me, and all I can do is shrug – because I truly have no idea what's going on.

As they make their way onto the stage, my attention is on the action at the back of the stage – and the moment I realize the kids have hijacked the practice drum set from the rehearsal room, and are quickly assembling it, I get a pretty good idea what they're up to. I also notice Cadi, standing silently in the shadows, grinning.

Everyone watches as Pete walks over and hands Emily her Stratocaster, and another quick glance at Cadi, makes me realize this is all her doing... *again*.

Finally, Patty walks over to Willie, grabbing a mic on her way.

"Mr. Morgan, these are the sticks you let me borrow a week ago. I'm returning them, with the hope you, and Ms. Táo, will join us for this last song – after all, it's because of you two that we managed to learn it."

The kids go nuts – there's no other way to describe it. I would never have believed that a couple hundred high school kids could possibly make this much noise! The other parents and teachers are as freaked as I am.

"*Let's rock this gym!*" Willie yells, taking a seat at the second drum set.

The lights go out, and in the near-total darkness, we hear the nifty little computer voice that begins the song, fill the gym – *with one little change...*

Hello
This is Stacie the computer

Good morning Stanley
I trust you slept well?
Will you be searching for true love today?

Even as everyone – including me – is laughing, I'm thinking up mean and devious things, to do to Cadi...

Two heartbeats later, the lights came up, and as everyone in the gym watches intently, Pete, Melinda, Patty and Sally – with a little help from the 'adults' – do exactly what they said they were going to do...

They destroy the place.

Patty and Willie in perfect unison.

Melinda and Emily, scorching out the lead riffs in with flawless timing.

Cadi thumping away on bass.

Pete hitting all the effect on his synthesizer, and keeping up with the keyboard rifts, at the same time.

And, of course, *all the girls* smoothly delivering back-up to Sally's squeaky, perfectly pitched, and insanely powerful voice, as she blows everyone away with her vocals.

It's just like Emma's performance in Southport – one of those things that you have to *see*. If you don't, there's simply no way anyone can ever explain it to you.

As the kids like to say... it is indeed, ***epic***.

Saturday Afternoon's performance tonight, will go down in the annals of Fort Collins High history.

When the song is over, the kids go completely nuts – again. I glance around and see Pete's dad and Patty's mom applauding louder than anyone in the building, and Sally's mom, actually in tears. The kids are standing center stage, high-fiving each other, as Willie, Cadi, and Emily jump off the stage, and walk toward me, getting high-fives from all the kids they pass.

Me… well… I'm so zoned, I'm numb.

When Willie, Cadi, and Emily stop in front of me, even in the semi-darkness, I can see the devious smirks on their faces.

I'm about to ask what they're up to when, without warning, the lights go out again, throwing the gym into total darkness, and creating a strange silence. Within seconds, we hear Sally's squeaky voice again fill the quiet void.

"We have one more song, and Mrs. Marshall was cool enough to give us permission at the last minute, to add it. Let's hear it for our principle!!"

The round of applause, and whistling that follows, would easily bury a decibel meter, had one been handy. I stand motionless in the midst of two hundred kids, and actually cover my ears – and of course, break up laughing. In the middle of the applause, a student walks up, taps Cadi on the shoulder, and when she leans over, the kid whispers something to her. She then nods at her, and turns back to face us.

"My presence is requested onstage again – seems they still need a bass player…" Cadi says, following it with a laugh. She hesitates for a heartbeat, then steps over to me, goes up on her tiptoes, and whispers in my ear… *"Hold on to your heart, Stanley Campbell…"*

We watch as she disappears into the darkness, in the direction of the stage. I look at Emily and Willie and am about to ask what's going on, when the gym is filled with a very familiar keyboard intro – and within seconds, I realize I'm going to cry, and there's nothing I can do about it.

That's when I notice it's still strangely silent – no cheering, or clapping – just Pete's keyboard intro.

Then, I hear her voice, as she sings those six magical lines – the intro to *Audio Distortion's* very first #1 song…

After the last line, there is again a hushed silence, and a single spotlight lands on me. As the tears slowly trickle down my cheeks, I feel a hand on my back…

When I turn around, there she is, smiling… and crying as well. She hands her mic to a kid standing next to her, wraps her arms around me, and squeezes me tighter than anyone ever has – in my entire life.

Then, with a single stroke of Melinda's guitar, the kids on stage – with Cadi's assistance – give the most awesome rendition of *Crazy Road* that I think I have ever heard.

Even as the kids break out dancing, Emma and I stand there, wrapped in each other's arms, totally oblivious to everything else.

Emma Greene is, and always has been… *my destiny*.

She is the love of my life.

thirty-four
Emma

The dance long over, we – the five of us – are standing around in Stan's classroom, watching Bailey teach Melissa how to play the drums. Stanley hasn't let go of my hand, since I wrapped my arms around him in the gym.

"So, you do realize you're back in the news, right, Emma?" Willie asks.

I turn and glare – playfully – at Cadi, who so far has been extremely quiet, and say, "Gee... wonder how *that* happened."

Cadi instantly blushes.

"Richard said he got no less than thirty phone calls about your 'impromptu performance' – in less than twenty-four hours," Stan says, laughing. "The first words out of his mouth were '*what the heck are you lunatics up to this time?*'"

"I think he's still miffed about our last show..." Emily says, making everyone laugh.

Cadi's comment – between laughs – is, "There is *no doubt* the girl can still sing, that's for certain."

"I saw the video – which I should mention went viral on YouTube in like forty-eight hours – and *you were amazing*, Emma," Emily offers, reaching out and poking me in the ribs. "Cadi's right, you *can* sing *anything*..."

"It's his fault you know..." I quickly point at Stan.

"Yeah," Emily says, trying not to laugh, "like *that* wasn't blatantly obvious?"

They all break up laughing, as I turn and kiss Stan on the cheek.

"So…" I offer, in the best devious tone I can muster, "if I'm going to be singing again, I'm going to need some music…"

Everyone – with the exception of the kids – freezes where they stand. As the four of them zone out for a moment, I glance at the girls, who are trying to climb up on a chair in front of Stanley's Roland. It takes them a few seconds, but they eventually end up side by side, pushing keys on the keyboard.

When Emily finally breaks the silence, I turn to look at her.

"Are you talking *performing*… or do you actually want to *record* again?"

"Well… that's kinda up to you guys… *My* schedule is pretty clear for the next…" I reply, fighting off a laugh.

And, as has been the case in my life – *actually our lives* – destiny is about to step in and screw with us.

I again glance at the kids, who are still standing on the chair, madly pushing every button they can find on the Roland, and laughing almost hysterically, which makes me start to laugh. Then, 'destiny' lets one of them find the 'right' button, and the room is suddenly filled with a *very* familiar background track, which is pretty much blasting from Stan's keyboard. Everyone turns to look at the same time, and the girls, thinking they're in trouble, jump down and run across the room to a drum set in the corner, and try to hide. Stan, laughing himself, immediately starts toward the keyboard, apparently intending to shut it down.

I, on the other hand, can't stop laughing…

"oh... my... god..." Emily mumbles, as Stan reaches up to power the keyboard down.

"NO, Stan! Wait!" Cadi yells at him.

In a single heartbeat, I understand. Each of them did exactly what I expected they would, when I sent them the CDs.

A very startled Stan jumps, stops laughing, and definitely a bit confused, turns and looks at us. Although he leaves the track playing, he turns the volume down considerably. Willie, never having said a single word, pushes his way between the kids, takes the sticks from his daughter, gently kisses her on the forehead, and then sits down, and to our total amazement, simply starts playing – matching the background track perfectly.

Within seconds, Cadi is playing the bass line, using a regular six string she found, to do it.

When, they reach a certain point, every head turns to look at Emily – who has an acoustic six string over her shoulder, and tears in her eyes. Without a word, she starts playing...

I grab my satchel, find my now tattered notebook, and open it to the page with the 'phantom CD' stuck in it. As I stand reading the lyrics on the page under the CD, I too begin to cry...

Destiny...

As soon as the four of them see my notebook, and my tears, they too, understand. I sit down, Indian style, on the floor, Bailey and Melissa rush over and drop to the floor next to me, and when the others loop back to the beginning of the track, I add the lyrics...

> *Begin again*
> *Discover friendships anew*
> *We will begin again*

> *Start a new journey home*
> *Now the time has come*
> *For five old friends to recall*
> *Where they all came from*
> *And why they must return home*

Once they hear my lyrics, Emily and Cadi start their own backup vocals, and of course, Melissa and Bailey join in as well. We go through the song slowly, four or five times, while Stan frantically scribbles notes non-stop. By the time we stop – more than an hour later – for the first time in close to four years, *Audio Distortion*, has created a *new* song.

More importantly, with the help of one very special guy, we've once again, found our way…

"Well guys…" Emily says, grinning and putting the guitar back in its case, "as weird as it was…"

"I'm pretty sure…" Cadi adds, doing the same with the guitar she was using.

"*Audio Distortion* just wrote…" comes from Willie, as he passes me, stopping to hand the drumsticks to his daughter.

"The *title song* for their new record…" Stan finally says, powering down the Roland.

"All we need now," I say, smiling at the four of them, "is permission to cover the track…"

They watch, as I pull the worn, gray cell phone from my satchel, flip it open, and dial a number.

"It's Emma Greene. Yes sir. Sorry for calling so early, but I needed to tell you… well… that it's done. Yes sir, just now, actually – it was totally impromptu. Uh-huh… all five of us. Well… Emily did make some small changes to the guitar portions, but other than that, it's intact. Yes sir. Well, we did cover *your music*, so ultimately, only you can say for sure, but *we* think it's *amazing*, and it perfectly fits our lives at this very moment. Yes sir. We'll be there. And thank you – for helping us find our way…"

As I close the phone, and lay it on the floor, Bailey come over, puts an arm around my shoulders, and whispers "*I like having an aunt,*" in my ear, and follows it with a giggle.

"So?" Emily asks.

"He's actually here – in the US – at the moment, and said he'll meet us in Richard's office, Thursday, next week, with the release. He's excited to hear what we've done with the song. I'll let him tell you why…"

"*Him?* You gonna tell us who he is?" Willie asks.

"A musician…" I reply, giving Willie a big smile, "who needed help from some other musicians. Turns out… we helped each other.

"Did he send us the CDs?" Emily asks.

"No… I did. He sent this…" I hold up the original phantom CD, "and I still have no idea how he found me. That's why I did what I did. I knew, deep in my heart, each of you would do exactly what you did… exactly what I did… *create.*"

"*Destiny…*" Cadi mumbles, staring right at me.

"So…" Stan says, also looking directly at me, as I stand up, "as my students so aptly put it to the principle the other day…"

Everyone laughs.

"…is *Audio Distortion* back together again, and is Mr. Campbell back to being a 'rock star'?"

Once again, the room is filled with laughter, including the fitful giggles of two little girls.

I walk over, and again hug Stanley. When I turn to look for the kids, I realize Cadi is, for some reason, the only person not laughing, and it's blatantly apparent she's desperately fighting her tears. I turn, take her hands in mine, and make her look at me.

"So... refresh my memory..." I start to say, but am interrupted as Cadi loses her battle with the tears.

"...we are, and always will be – no matter what paths we travel, or what complications life throws at us – Audio Distortion," she softly mumbles, between her building sobs.

The others fall silent, and turn to look at her, each understanding what she's done.

Cadi has accomplished in three weeks, what each of us has silently *wanted* to do, for at least the last year – if not longer.

The look in her eyes at this exact moment makes me realize that *everything* she's done, since the day she called Stanley, has had a singular purpose – *to bring the five of us to this moment.*

Her true intent – whether subconsciously or consciously – from the beginning, was to reunite *Audio Distortion*.

But more importantly, she fully intended to get the five of us to rekindle the friendships, we should have been sharing all along.

My heart now racing, I squat down, and pick up a grinning and giggling Bailey, who has spent the last few moments, gently tugging on my dress. After a few more seconds of total silence, I turn and look at Stan, who grins and looks at Emily, who shrugs and looks at Willie, who laughs and puts an arm around Cadi.

"If Richard thought we were up to something before, wait until he hears about all this..." I offer, carefully watching my friend's faces.

When no one says anything, it makes me laugh – loudly – and prompts me to do the one thing none of us ever expected we would do together again.

Grinning like a kid, I put Bailey down, and stick my arms out in front me, hands open...

Not a single one of them hesitates...

Not even slightly...

One at time, we make our pre-show Star...

Emily steps up on my right, a huge grin on her face, and extends her arms as well. Stanley steps into the circle facing us, and takes my left hand with his right, and Emily's right, with his left. In seconds, Willie joins us, and with a laugh, takes my right hand in his left.

"Yes, Stanley," I say, as Cadi steps in to complete the Star, taking Emily's left hand, with her right, and Willie's right with her left, "I'm pretty sure 'Mr. Campbell is back to being a *rock star*'..."

When we pull our hands back and yell... I think we probably woke up half the city...

epilogue

A WEEK LATER
ON THE FRONT STEPS OF STANLEY'S HOUSE

Emma

"I want to ask something, but I don't want to be rude…"

"You can always ask me anything, Georgia."

She hesitates, and gives me an odd look.

"Are you okay now? Is your head straight?"

"Well…" I reply, laughing, "is anyone ever truly 'straight'?

Again, I get that odd, and slightly quizzical look. I put an arm around her shoulders, and squeeze.

"Yes, Georgia, I'm straight. Straighter than I have ever been in my entire life. I'm hoping your brother gets off his butt and pops the question – soon. I'm ready to be Mrs. Campbell…"

"I think you need to be the liberated woman."

"You think I should ask him?"

"No… I think you should TELL him."

I try to wrap my brain around Georgia's idea.

"Hummm… Get tickets, get him, fly to Reno…"

"…and *get married*," she blurts out, finishing my thought. "You're catching on, Sis!"

I laugh, lean over, and hug her.

"Come on girl – give me the 'Stan's House' tour."

We stand up, Georgia unlocks the door, we go inside, and down a short hall, where I see at least three old photos of the band, hanging on the walls.

When we reach the end of the hall, Georgia is about to turn toward the kitchen, when something in the living room, grabs my attention.

It's a framed photograph, sitting alone on a table.

Without a word, I turn, cross the room and pick it up. A now nervous Georgia is quick to follow me.

"No way..." I blurt out, as I stare at it.

"Uh..."

"Oh hush, Georgia," I reply, turning and glancing at her, then going back to the photograph. "Your brother had a girlfriend. Big deal. Do you think I was alone for three years?"

When she doesn't respond, I again turn to look at her. Talk about 'confused and concerned' – it's hard to say which is more prominent on the girl's face.

"Who is she?" I ask, looking back at the photo.

Georgia is about to answer me, when I have a change of mind, and cut her off.

"No... wait. Don't tell me. I need a pair of scissors, Georgia."

Georgia shrugs, turns to a desk behind her, and in seconds produces a pair scissors. I turn, sit down on the couch, and pull what was once a notebook, out of my laptop bag. It takes me a few moments to find what I want, and the moment I do, I get goose bumps. I pull out the photo, and as Georgia comes around the couch, I hold it up so she can see it.

"Wanna see 'weird'?"

Georgia looks first at the photo I'm holding up, then at the one in the frame, then back at mine.

"No freakin' way, Emma!"

I laugh, take the scissors, and start cutting my photo in half – at a very specific spot. As I'm doing it, we hear the front door open, and then close.

"Hey guys – you in here?" Stanley calls out.

Seconds later, having gotten no response, Stanley appears in the doorway across from us. One look at the two of us, and his smile disappears.

"Uh... hey guys... what's going on?"

Having cut my photo, I'm disassembling the framed photo, as I turn to look at Stan.

"Who took this photo, Stanley?"

"Huh?"

I laugh, and glance at Georgia, who at this point, has figured out what I'm doing.

"I said... who took this photo?"

"Uh... well..."

"Quit weirding out, and answer the question."

Georgia lets out a laugh, as I finish my task and turn the frame back over. Her response is instant...

"No way! Seriously? How is that even possible?"

Stan, now as curious as he is nervous, crosses the room, stops behind us, and stands looking over my shoulder.

"An old guy... A strange, pushy, old guy..." Stan mumbles.

"Okay... does this sound familiar? Long gray ponytail? Spoke with a bizarre accent? *Insisted* he needed to take the photo? *Insisted* you guys stand in a very specific spot?"

Georgia, holding the framed photo, sits silently, and still looks totally confused. Stanley looks like he may actually faint.

"How in God's name would you know that?"

I smile, again open my notebook, pull out one of three slightly different versions of the photo I just cut up, and hand it to him.

"*Because...* the nut did the exact same thing to us. It took the obnoxious old fart, three tries and twenty minutes of moving us around, before he was satisfied. Then, without a word, he disappeared."

There's a bizarre, hushed silence, for a few seconds, and then I take the framed photo from Georgia, and hand it to Stanley as well.

Stan finds himself staring at photograph of Christopher with his arm around the girl in his photo, standing under the Eiffel Tower. I inserted the half of *my* photo that contained Christopher, over the half of the photo in the frame that has Stan in it. The bizarrely strange thing is, one fit over the other, so perfectly, that the image in the frame now appears to be an *unaltered photograph*.

After staring at the two images – the photo I handed him, and the altered photos in the frame – for a few seconds, Stan's shocked look becomes even more pronounced. Georgia notices it immediately…

"Stan? What's wrong?" his sister asks.

Stan looks at her, and then hands the frame back to me.

"Look at the *date*, Emma…"

I reach out, take the frame, and when I glance at the lower right hand corner, where the date and time were digitally imprinted by the camera, I get it. I pick up the cut-off half of my photo, which is still lying in my lap, look at it, and start laughing.

"What's going on?" Georgia asks, leaning toward me.

I hand both the frame, and the half-photo, to her. She takes them, her eyes move immediately to the date stamps, and the girl almost loses it.

"*Oh… my… God…*" she whispers.

The date and time on both photographs is in a twenty-four hour format. Stan's photo shows it was taken on 7/7 at 17:00 – which is 5:00 PM. The stamp on my photo is 7/7 at 17:17.

If one is to believe the timestamps – which I'm honestly not sure I do – not only were the four of us *in Paris at the same time*, but we were standing in the *same spot,* separated by seventeen minutes.

And we never saw each other…

I look up at Stanley, who smiles at me, because he too, now understands.

"Her name is Courtney, and she went back to Boston, looking for a guy named Christopher…"

"His name is Christopher, and I'm thinking he's in Boston, looking for a girl named Courtney…" Stanley instantly replies.

"Okay guys…" Georgia says, her voice cracking, "…this is like twilight zone stuff. First of all, how in the heck would you guys know their names, *and,* how is *any of this* even possible?"

Without responding to Georgia, I stand up, walk around the couch, wrap my arms around Stan, and hug him tighter than I ever have. After a second, I step back, and with tears in my eyes, again look up at him.

"It was never about us, Stanley…"

He smiles, reaches out, and wipes the tears off my cheeks.

"It was always about the two of them…"

He pauses, and gently kisses me.

"all of it…" he whispers.

"So…" I ask, a big grin on my face, "What's your position on the whole 'destiny' thing now, Stanley Campbell?"

He smiles and again hugs me. When he lets me go, I step back, and turn to find a very confused Georgia.

"I'll try to explain it all later – I promise," I say, giving her a big grin.

"Do you think they found each other?" Stan asks, still holding tightly to one of my hands.

"Without a doubt, Stanley... *without a doubt*. The photos are *His* way of telling us they did..."

Reunited and headed for their
greatest accomplishment yet!

Coming Soon!

All About The Music

The wildest chapter so far, in the lives of
Emma, Stanley, Emily, Willie, and Cadi.

Known to the world as...

AUDIO DISTORTION

The band critics say
'never seems to go away'

Available in print and digital formats online
audio-distortion.com
amazon.com

Made in the USA
San Bernardino, CA
04 August 2016